Laura Elizabeth Howe Richards

Nautilus

Laura Elizabeth Howe Richards

Nautilus

ISBN/EAN: 9783337395971

Printed in Europe, USA, Canada, Australia, Japan

Cover: Foto ©Andreas Hilbeck / pixelio.de

More available books at **www.hansebooks.com**

BY

LAURA E. RICHARDS

AUTHOR OF "CAPTAIN JANUARY," "MELODY," "MARIE," "QUEEN
HILDEGARDE," ETC., ETC.

Illustrated

BOSTON
ESTES AND LAURIAT
1895

TO MY DEAR FRIENDS,

THE MEMBERS OF THE

HOWE CLUB,

OF GARDINER, MAINE,

THIS STORY IS AFFECTIONATELY

DEDICATED.

CONTENTS.

NAUTILUS

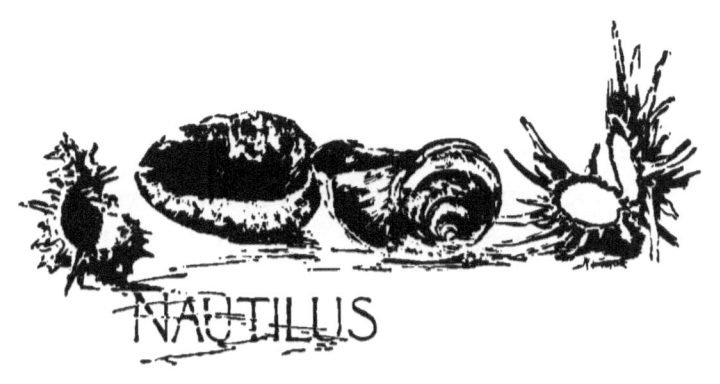

NAUTILUS

CHAPTER I.

THE boy John was sitting on the wharf, watching the ebb of the tide. The current was swift, for there had been heavy rains within a few days; the river was full of drifting logs, bits of bark, odds and ends of various kinds; the water, usually so blue, looked brown and thick. It swirled round the great mossy piers, making eddies between them; from time to time the boy dropped bits of paper into these eddies, and saw with delight how they spun round and round, like living things, and finally gave up the struggle and were borne away down stream.

"Only, in the real maelstrom," he said, "they don't be carried away; they go over the edge, down into the black hole, whole ships and ships, and you never see them again.

I wonder where they stop, or whether it goes through to the other side of the world."

A great log came drifting along, and struck against a pier; the end swung round, and it rested for a few moments, beating against the wooden wall. This, it was evident, was a wrecked vessel, and it behooved the boy John, as a hero and a life-saver, to rescue her passengers. Seizing a pole, he lay down on his stomach and carefully drew the log toward him, murmuring words of cheer the while.

"They are almost starved to death!" he said, piti-fully. "The captain is tied to the mast, and they have not had anything to eat but boots and a puppy for three weeks. The mate and some of the sailors took all the boats and ran away,—at least, not ran, but went off and left the rest of 'em; and they have all said their prayers, for they are very good folks, and the captain did n't *want* to kill the puppy one bit, but he had to, or else they would all be dead now. And—and the reckoning was dead,—I wonder what that means, and why it is dead so often,—and so they could n't tell where they were, but they knew that there were cannibals on *almost* all the islands, and this was the hungriest time of the year for cannibals."

Here followed a few breathless moments, during which the captain, his wife and child, and the faithful members of the crew, were pulled up to the wharf by the unaided arm of the boy John. He wrapped them in hot blankets and gave them brandy and peanut taffy: the first because it was what they always did in books; the second because it was the best thing in the world, and would take away the nasty taste of the brandy.

Leaving them in safety, and in floods of grateful tears, the rescuer bent over the side of the wharf once more, intent on saving the gallant ship from her fate; but at this moment came a strong swirl of tide, the log swung round once more and floated off, and the rescuer fell "all along" into the water. This was nothing unusual, and he came puffing and panting up the slippery logs, and sat down again, shaking himself like a Newfoundland puppy. He wished the shipwrecked crew had not seen him; he knew he should get a whipping when he reached home, but that was of less consequence. Anyhow, she was an old vessel, and now the captain would get a new ship — a fine one, full rigged, with new sails as white as snow; and on his next voyage he would take him, the boy John, in place of the faithless mate, and they would sail away, away, down the river and far across the ocean, and then, — then he would hear the sound of the sea. After all, you never could hear it in the river, though that was, oh, so much better than nothing! But the things that the shells meant when they whispered, the things that the wind said over and over in the pine trees, those things you never could know until you heard the real sound of the real sea.

The child rose and stretched himself wearily. He had had a happy time, but it was over now; he must leave the water, which he cared more for than for anything in the world, — must leave the water and go back to the small close house, and go to bed, and dream no more dreams.

Ah! when would some one come, — no play hero, but a real one, in a white-sailed ship, and carry him off, never to set foot on shore again?

He turned to go, for the shadows were falling, and already a fog had crept up the river, almost hiding the brown, swiftly-flowing water; yet before leaving the wharf he turned back once more and looked up and down, with eyes that strove to pierce the fog veil, — eager, longing eyes of a child, who hopes every moment to see the doors open into fairy-land.

And lo! what was this that he saw? What was this that came gliding slowly, silently out of the dusk, out of the whiteness, itself whiter than the river fog, more shadowy than the films of twilight? The child held his breath, and his heart beat fast, fast. A vessel, or the ghost of a vessel? · Nearer and nearer it came, and now he could see masts and spars, sails spread to catch the faint breeze, gleaming brass-work about the decks. A vessel, surely; yet, — what was that? The fog lifted for a moment, or else his eyes grew better used to the dimness, and he saw a strange thing. On the prow of the vessel, which now was seen to be a schooner, stood a figure; a statue, was it? Surely it was a statue of bronze, like the Soldiers' Monument, leaning against the mast, with folded arms.

Nearer! Fear seized the boy, for he thought the statue had eyes like real eyes, and he saw them move, as if looking from right to left; the whites glistened, the dark balls rolled from side to side. The child stood still, feeling as if he had called up this phantom out of his own thoughts;

perhaps in another minute it would fade away into the fog, as it had come, and leave only the flowing tide and the shrouded banks on either side!

Nearer! and now the bronze figure lifted its arm, slowly, silently, and pointed at the boy. But this was more than flesh and blood could stand; little John uttered a choking cry, and turning his back on the awful portent, ran home as fast as he could lay foot to ground. And on seeing this the bronze figure laughed, and its teeth glistened, even as the eyes had done.

CHAPTER II.

THE SKIPPER.

THE little boy slept brokenly that night. Bronze statues flitted through his dreams, sometimes frowning darkly on him, folding him in an iron clasp, dragging him down into the depths of roaring whirlpools; sometimes, still stranger to say, smiling, looking on him with kindly eyes, and telling him that the sea was not so far away as he thought, and that one day he should see it and know the sound of it. His bed was a white schooner,—there seemed no possible doubt of that; it tossed up and down as it lay by the wharf; and once the lines were cast off, and he was about to be carried away, when up rose the crew that he had rescued from shipwreck, and cried with one voice, " No! no! he shall not go!" The voice was that of Mr. Endymion Scraper, and not a pleasant voice to hear; moreover, the voice had hands, lean and hard, which clutched the boy's shoulder, and shook him roughly; and at last, briefly, it appeared that it was time to get up, and that if the boy John did not get up that minute, like the lazy good-for-nothing he was, Mr. Scraper would give him such a lesson as he would not forget for one while.

John tumbled out of bed, and stood rubbing his eyes for a moment, his wits still abroad. The water heaved and subsided under him, but presently it hardened into the garret floor. He staggered a few steps, as the hard hand gave him a push and let him go, then stood firm and looked about him. Gradually the room grew familiar ; the painted bed and chair, the window with its four small panes, which he loved to polish and clean, " so that the sky could come through," the purple mussel-shell and the china dog, his sole treasures and ornaments. The mussel was his greatest joy, perhaps ; it had been given him by a fisherman, who had brought a pocket-full back from his sea trip, to please his own children. It made no sound, but the tint was pure and lovely, and it was lined with rainbow pearl. The dog was not jealous, for he knew (or the boy John thought he knew), that he was, after all, the more companionable of the two, and that he was talked to ten times for the mussel's once. John was telling him now, as he struggled into his shirt and trousers, about the vision of last night, and the dreams that followed it. " And as soon as ever I have my chores done," he said, and his eyes shone, and his cheek flushed at the thought, " as soon as ever, I'm going down there, just to see. Of course, I suppose it isn't there, you know ; but then, — if it should be ! "

The dog expressed sympathy in his usual quiet way, and was of the opinion that John should go by all means, for, after all, who could say that the vision might not have been reality? When one considered the stories one had read! and had not the dog just heard the whole of " Robinson Crusoe " read aloud, bit by bit, in stealthy whispers, by early daylight, by moonlight, by stray bits of candle begged from a neighbor,—had he not heard and appreciated every word of the immortal story? He was no ignorant dog, indeed! His advice was worth having.

Breakfast was soon eaten; it did not take long to eat breakfast in Mr. Scraper's house. The chores were a more serious matter, for every spoon and plate had to be washed to the tune of a lashing tongue, and under an eye that withered all it lighted on. But at last,—at last the happy hour came when the tyrant's back was turned, and the tyrant's feet tottered off in the direction of the post-office. The daily purchases, the daily gossip at the " store," would fill the rest of the morning, as John well knew. He listened in silence to the charges to " keep stiddy to work, and git that p'tater-patch wed by noon; " he watched the departure of his tormentor, and went straight to the potato-patch, duty and fear leading him by either hand. The weeds had no safety of their lives that day; he was in too great a hurry to dally, as he loved to do, over the bigger stalks of pigweed, the giants which he, with his trusty sword — only it was a hoe — would presently dash to the earth and behead, and tear in pieces. Even the sprawling pusley-stems, which generally played the part of devil-fish and tarantulas and various other monsters, suffered no amputation of limb by limb, but were torn up with merciful haste, and flung in heaps together.

Was the potato-patch thoroughly " wed?" I hardly know. But I know that in less than an hour after Mr. Endymion Scraper started for the village the boy John was on his way to the wharf.

As he drew near the river he found that something was the matter with his breath. It would not come regularly, but in gasps and sighs; his heart beat so hard, and was so high up in his throat he was almost choked. Would he see anything when he turned the corner that led down to the wharf? And if anything,—what? Then he shut his eyes and turned the corner.

The schooner was there. No longer spectral or shadowy, she lay in plain sight by the wharf, her trim lines pleasant to look at, her decks shining with neatness, her canvas all spread out to dry, for the night dew had been heavy. Lifting his fearful eyes, the child saw the bronze figure standing in the bow, but now it was plainly seen to be a man, a swarthy man, with close-curled black hair, and bright, dark eyes. Two other men were lounging about the deck, but John took little heed of them. This man, the strangest he had ever seen, claimed his whole thought. He was as dark as the people in the geography book, where the pictures of the different races were; not an Ethiopian, evidently (John loved the long words in the geography book), because his nose was straight and his lips thin; perhaps a Malay or an Arab. If one could see a real Arab, one could ask him about the horses, and whether the dates were always sticky, and what he did in a sandstorm, and lots of interesting things. And then a Malay, — why, you could ask him how he felt when he ran amuck, — only, perhaps, that would not be polite.

These meditations were interrupted by a hail from the schooner. It was the dark man himself who spoke, in a quiet voice that sounded kind.

" Good - morning, sir! Will you come aboard this morning ? "

John was not used to being called " Sir," and the word fell pleasantly on ears that shrank from the detested syllable " Bub," with which strangers were wont to greet him.

" Yes, if you please," he answered, with some dignity. It is, perhaps, difficult to be stately when one is only five feet tall, but John felt stately inside, as well as shy. The stranger turned and made a sign to the other men, who came quickly, bringing a gang-plank, which they ran out from the schooner's deck to the wharf. The Skipper, for such the dark man appeared to be, made a sign of invitation, and after a moment's hesitation, John ran across and stood on the deck of the white schooner. Was he still dreaming ? Would he wake in a moment and find himself back in the garret at home, with Mr. Scraper shaking him ?

" Welcome, young gentleman ! " said the Skipper, holding out his hand. " Welcome ! the first visitor to the schooner. That it is a child, brings luck for the next voyage, so we owe you a thank. We arrived last night only. And what is my young gentleman's name ? "

" My name is John," said the boy, standing with downcast eyes before this wonderful person.

" And mine ! " said the Skipper, — " two Johns, the black and the red. You should be called Juan Colorado, for your hair of red gold."

The boy looked up quickly, his cheek flushing; he did not like to be laughed at; but the Skipper's face was perfectly grave, and only courtesy and hospitality shone from his dark eyes.

" I wonder what the schooner's name is!" John said, presently, speaking low, and addressing his remarks apparently to the mast, which he kicked gently with his foot.

" The schooner is the ' Nautilus,' young gentleman ! "

The reply came from the Skipper, not from the mast, yet it was still to the latter that the boy made his next observation.

" I wonder where she comes from, and where she is going, and what she is going to do here!" And having delivered himself breathlessly of these remarks, the boy John wished he could squeeze through a port-hole, or melt away into foam, or get away somehow, anyhow.

But now he felt himself lifted in strong arms, and set on the rail of the vessel, with his eyes just opposite those of the Skipper, so that he could not look up without meeting them ; and on so looking up, it became evident immediately that this was the kindest man in the world, and that he liked boys, and that, finally, there was nothing to be afraid of. On which John heaved a mighty sigh of relief, and then smiled, and then laughed.

" I like to know things !" he said, simply.

" Me, too," replied the Skipper. " I also like to know things. How else shall we become wise, Juan Colorado ? Now listen, and you shall hear. This schooner is the ' Nautilus,' as I say, and she is a Spanish schooner. Yes ; " (in reply to the question in the boy's eyes,) " I am partly a

Spanish man, but not all. I have other mankind in me, young gentleman. We come from the Bahamas. Do you know where are they, the Bahamas?"

John nodded. He liked geography, and stood at the head of his class. "Part of the West Indies," he said, rapidly. "Low, coral islands. One of them, San Salvador, is said to be the first land discovered by Columbus in 1492. Principal exports, sugar, coffee, cotton, tobacco, and tropical fruits. Belong to Great Britain. That's all I know."

"Caramba!" said a handsome youth, who was lounging on the rail a few feet off, gazing on with idle eyes, "you got the schoolmaster here, Patron! I did not know all that, me, and I come, too, from Bahamas. Say, you teach a school, M'sieur?"

"Franci!" said the Patron, gravely.

"Si, Señor!" said Franci, with a beautiful smile, which showed his teeth under his black mustache.

"There is a school of flying-fish in the cabin. Better see to them!"

"Si, Señor!" said Franci, and disappeared down the hatchway.

"Is there?" asked the boy John, with great eyes of wonder. The Skipper smiled, and shook his head.

"Franci understands me," he said. "I wish to tell him that he go about his business, and not linger,— as you say, loaf about the deck. I take a little way round about, but he understands very well, Franci. And of all these exports, what does the young gentleman think I have brought from the Bahamas?"

"I — I was just wondering!" John confessed; but he did not add his secret hope that it was something more interesting than cotton or tobacco.

The Skipper turned and made a quick, graceful gesture with his hand. "Perhaps the young gentleman like to see my cargo," he said. "Do me the favor!" and he led the way down to the cabin.

Now it became evident to the boy that all had indeed been a dream. It sometimes happened that way, dreaming that you woke and found it all true, and then starting up to find that the first waking had been of dream-stuff too, that it was melting away from your sight, from your grasp; even things that looked so real, so real, — he pinched himself violently, and shook his head, and tried to break loose from fetters of sleep, binding him to such sweet wonders, that he must lose next moment; but no waking came, and the wonders remained.

The cabin was full of shells. Across one end of the little room ran a glazed counter, where lay heaped together various objects of jewelry, shell necklaces, alligator teeth and sea-beans set in various ways, tortoise-shell combs, bracelets and hairpins, — a dazzling array. Yet the boy's eyes passed almost carelessly over these treasures, to light with quick enchantment on the shells themselves, the *real* shells, as he instantly named them to himself, resenting half-consciously the turning of Nature's wonders into objects of vulgar adornment.

The shells were here, the shells were there, the shells were all around! Shelf above shelf of them, piled in heaps, lying in solitary splendor, arranged in patterns, — John had never, in his wildest dreams, seen so many shells. Half the poetry of his little life had been in the lovely forms and colors that lay behind the locked glass doors in Mr. Scraper's parlor; for Mr. Scraper was a collector of shells in a small way. John had supposed his collection to be, if not the only one in the world, at least the most magnificent, by long odds ; yet here were the old man's precious units multiplied into tens, into twenties, sometimes into hundreds, and all lying open to the day, as if anyone, even a small one, even a little boy, who almost never had anything in his hand more precious than his own purple mussel at home, might touch and handle them and feel himself in heaven.

They gleamed with the banded glories of the rainbow ; they softened into the moonlight beauty of the pearl ; they veiled their loveliness in milky clouds, through which the color showed as pure and sweet as the cheek of a bride ; they glowed with depths of red and flame that might almost burn to the touch.

The little boy stood with clasped hands, and sobbed with excitement. " Did you dig up all the sea ?". he asked, in a wonder that was not without reproach. " Are there none left any more, at all ? "

The Skipper laughed quietly. " The mermaids see not any difference, sir," he said. " Where I take one shell from its rock, I leave a hundred, a thousand. The sea is a good mother, she has plenty children. See! " he added, lifting a splendid horned shell, " this is the Royal

Triton. On a rock I found him, twenty fathom down. It was a family party, I think, for all around they lay, some clinging to the rock, some in the mud, some walking about. I take one, two, three, put them in my pouch; up I go, and the others, they have a little more room, that's all."

John's eyes glowed in his head.

" I — I should like to see that!" he cried. " What is it like down there? Do sharks come by, — swish! with their great tails? And why don't they eat you, like the man in the geography book? And is there really a sea-serpent? And do the oysters open and shut their mouths, so that you can see the pearls, or how do you know which are the right ones?

"There are a great many things that I have thought about all my life," he said, " and nobody could ever tell me. The bottom of the sea, that is what I want most in the world to know about."

He paused, out of breath, and would have been abashed at his own boldness, had not the Skipper's eyes told him so perfectly that they had understood all about it, and that there was no sort of reason why he should not ask all the questions he liked.

They were wonderful eyes, those of the Skipper. Most black eyes are wanting in the depths that one sounds in blue, or gray, in brown, more rarely in hazel eyes; they flash with an outward brilliancy, they soften into velvet, but one seldom sees through them into the heart. But these eyes, though black beyond a doubt, had the darkness of deep, still water, when you look into it and see the surface mantling with a bluish gloss, and beneath that depth upon depth of black — clear, serene, unfathomable. And when a smile came into them, — ah, well! we all know how that same dark water looks when the sun strikes on it. The sun struck now, and little John felt warm and comfortable all through his body and heart.

"The bottom of the sea?" said the Skipper, taking up a shell and polishing it on his coat-sleeve. "Yes, that is a fine place, Colorado. You mind not that I call you Colorado? It pleases me, — the name. A fine place, truly. You have never seen the sea, young gentleman?"

The boy shook his head.

"Never, really!" he said. "I — I've dreamed about it a great deal, and I think about it most of the time. There's a picture in my geography book, just a piece of sea, and then broken off, so that you don't see any end to it; that makes it seem real, somehow, I don't know why.

"But I've heard the sound of it!" he added, his face brightening. "There's a shell in Mr. Scraper's parlour, on the mantelpiece, and sometimes when he goes to sleep I can get it for a minute, and hold it to my ear, and then I hear the sound, the sound of the sea."

"Yes," said the Skipper, taking up another shell from one of the shelves, a tiger cowry, rich with purple and brown. "The sound of the sea; that is a good thing. Listen here, young gentleman, and tell me what the tiger say to you of the sea."

He held the shell to the boy's ear, and saw the colour

and the light come like a wave into his face. They were
silent for a moment; then the child spoke, low and
dreamily.

"It does n't say words, you know!" he said. "It's just
a soft noise, like what the pine-trees make, but it sounds
cool and green and—and wet. And there are waves a
long way off, curling over and over, and breaking on
white beaches, and they smell good and salt. And it
seems to make me know about things down under the sea,
and bright colours shining through the water, and light
coming 'way down—cool, green light, that does n't make
you wink when you look at it. And—and I guess there
are lots of fishes swimming about, and their eyes shine,
too, and they move just as soft, and do n't make any noise,
no more than if their mother was sick in the next room.
And on the ground there seem to be like flowers, only
they move and open and shut without any one touching
them. And—and—"

Was the boy going into a trance? Were the dark eyes
mesmerizing him, or was all this to be heard in the shell?
The Skipper took the shell gently from his hand, and
stroked his hair once or twice, quickly and lightly.
"That will do!" he said. "The young gentleman can
hear truly. All these things are under the sea, yes, and
more, oh, many more! Some day you shall see them,
young gentleman; who knows? But now comes Franci
to make the dinner. Will Señor Colorado dine with the
Skipper from the Bahamas? Welcome he will be, truly."

Little John started, and a guilty flush swept over his
clear face.

"I forgot!" he cried. "I forgot all about everything, and Cousin Scraper will be home by this time, and — and — I 'll have to be going, please; but I 'll come again, if you think I may."

The Skipper had raised his eyebrows at the name of Scraper, and was now looking curiously at the boy. "Who is that you say?" he asked. "Scraper, your cousin? And of your father, young gentleman, — why do you not speak of him?"

"My father is dead," replied little John. "And my mother too, a good while ago. I do n't remember father. Mother—" he broke off, and dropped his eyes to hide the tears that sprang to them. "Mother died a year ago," he said ; "ever since then I 've lived with Cousin Scraper. He 's some sort of kin to father, and he says he 's my guardian by law."

"His other name?" suggested the dark man, quietly. "For example, Endymion?"

"Why, yes!" cried John, raising his honest blue eyes in wonder. "Do you know him, sir? Have you ever been here before?"

The Skipper shook his head. "Not of my life!" he said. "Yet — I make a guess at the name; perhaps of this gentleman I have heard. He — he is a kind person, Colorado?"

John hung his head. He knew that he must not speak evil ; his mother had always told him that ; yet what else was there to speak about Cousin Scraper? "He — he collects shells!" he faltered, after a pause, during which he was conscious of the Skipper's eyes piercing through and through him, and probably seeing the very holes in his stockings. But now the Skipper threw back his head with a laugh.

"He collects shells, eh? My faith, I have come to the right place, I with my ' Nautilus.' See, young gentleman! I go with my shells where I think is good market. In large cities, many rich people who collect shells. I sell many, many, some very precious. Never have I come up this river of great beauty; but I say, who knows? Maybe here are persons who know themselves, who have the feeling of shells in their hearts. I find, first you, Colorado; and that you have the feeling in your heart I see, at the first look you give to my pretties here. That you have the fortune to live with a collector, that I could not guess, ha? He is kind, I say, this Scraper? He loves you as a son, he gives you his shells to look at, to care for as your own?"

John hung his head again.

"He keeps them locked up," he admitted. "I never had one in my hand, except the one on the mantelpiece, sometimes when he goes to sleep after dinner. I — I must be going now!" he cried in desperation, making his way to the gang-plank. "I must get home, or he'll — "

"What he will do?" the Skipper inquired, holding the plank in his hand. "What he do to you, young gentleman, eh? A little scold you, because you stay too long to talk with the Skipper from the Bahamas, hey? No more than that, is it not?"

"He'll beat me," cried little John, driven fairly past himself. "He beats me every time I'm late, or do n't get my work done. I thank you ever so much for being so kind, but I can't stay another minute."

"Adios, then, Señor Colorado!" said the Skipper, with a stately bow. "You come soon again, I pray you. And if you will tell Sir Scraper, and all those others, your friends, the shell schooner is here. Exhibition in a few hours ready, free to all. Explanation and instruction when desired by intelligent persons desiring of to know the habits under the sea. Schooner 'Nautilus,' from the Bahamas, with remarkable collection of shells and marine curiosities. Adios, Señor Juan Colorado!"

CHAPTER III.

A GREAT EXHIBITION.

L ITTLE JOHN was not the one to spread the tidings of the schooner's arrival. He had to take his whipping, — a hard one it was! — and then he was sent down into the cellar to sift ashes, as the most unpleasant thing that could be devised for a fine afternoon. But the news spread, for all that. John was not the only boy in the village of Tidewater, and by twelve o'clock every man, woman and child was talking about the new arrival ; and by two o'clock, the dinner dishes being put away, and the time of the evening chores still some hours off, nearly every man, woman and child was hastening in the direction of the wharf. Of course the boys were going. It was vacation time, and what else should boys do but see all that was to be seen ? And of course it was the duty of the elders to see that the children came to no harm. So the fathers were strolling leisurely down, saying to each other that 't was all nonsense, most likely, and nothing worth seeing, but some one ought to be looking out that the boys and the women folks did n't get cheated. The mothers were putting on their bonnets, in the serene consciousness that if anyone was going to be cheated it was not they, and that goodness knew what those men-folks would be up to on that schooner if they were left to themselves. And

33

the little girls were shaking the pennies out of their money boxes, or if they had no boxes, watching with eager eyes their more fortunate sisters. Truly, it was a great day in the village.

The Skipper welcomed one and all. He stood by the gang-plank, and Franci stood by him, cap in hand, smiling in a beautiful way. On the rail were perched two little monkeys, their arms round each other's shoulders, their bright eyes watching with eager curiosity all that went on. When the Skipper bowed, they bowed; when he smiled, they grinned; and when he put out his hand to help a woman or a child aboard, they laid their hands on their hearts, and tried to look like Franci. The Skipper was their lord and master, and they loved and feared him, and did his bidding as often as their nature would allow; but in the depths of their little monkey hearts they cherished a profound admiration for Franci, and they were always hoping that this time they were looking like him when they smiled. (But they never were!)

The only other visible member of the crew was a long, lazy-looking Yankee, whom the Skipper called Rento, and the others plain " Rent," his full name of Laurentus Woodcock being more than they could away with. But it was not to see the crew, neither the schooner (though she was a pretty schooner enough, as anybody who knew about such matters could see), that the village had come out; it was to see the exhibition, and the exhibition was ready for them. An awning was spread over the after-deck, and under this was arranged with care the main collection of corals and shells, the commoner sorts, such as found a ready sale at low prices. There was pure white coral, in long branches, studded with tiny points, like the wraith of the fairy thorn; there were great piles of the delicate fan-coral, which the sailors call sea-fans, and which Franci would hold out to every girl who had any pretence to good looks, with his most gracious bow, and " Young lady like to fan herself, keep the sun off, *here* you air, ladies!" While Laurentus would blush and hang his head if any woman addressed him, and would murmur the wrong price in an unintelligible voice if the woman happened to be young and pretty.

Then there were mushroom corals, so inviting that one could hardly refrain from carrying them home and cooking them for tea; and pincushion corals, round and hard, look-ing as if they had been stolen from the best bedroom of some uncompromising New England mermaid. Yes; there was no end to the corals. The lovely white branches were cheap, and nearly every child went off with a branch, small or large, dwelling on it with eyes of rapture, seeing noth-ing else in the world, in some cases failing to see even the way, and being rescued from peril of water by the Skipper or Rento. The favourite shells were the conches, of all sizes and varieties, from the huge pink-lipped Tritons of the " Triumph of Galatea," down to fairy things, many-whorled, rainbow-tinted, which were included in the " handful for five cents " which Franci joyously proclaimed at intervals, when he thought the children looked wistful and needed cheering up, since they could not have all they saw.

But the Cypræas were beautiful, too, and of every colour, from white or palest amber to deep sullen purples and browns that melted into ebony. These were the shells with voices, that spoke of the sea; many a child raised them to his ear, and listened with vague delight to the far-away, uncertain murmur; but not to every child is it given to hear the sound of the sea, and it may be doubted whether any boy or girl would have understood what the boy John meant, if he had declared the things that the shell had said to him.

Where was John? Franci and Rento had charge of the deck exhibition, but the Skipper kept his station at the head of the gang-plank, and while courteously receiving his visitors, with a word of welcome for each, he looked often up the road to see if his little friend was coming. He thought the gleam of red hair would brighten the landscape; but it came not, and the Skipper was not one to neglect a possible customer. Now and again he would touch some one on the arm, and murmur gently, "In a few moments presently, other exhibition in the cabin, to which I have the pleasure of invite you. I attend in person, which is free to visitors."

He spoke without accent, the Skipper, but his sentences were sometimes framed on foreign models, and it was no wonder if now and then he met a blank stare. He looked a little bored, possibly; these faces, full of idle wonder, showed no trace of the collector's eager gaze; yet he was content to wait, it appeared. Mr. Bill Hen Pike judged, from the way in which everything was trigged up, that the schooner "cal'lated to make some stay here-abouts;" and the Skipper did not contradict him, but bowed gravely, and said, "In a few moments, gentleman, do me the honour to descend to the cabin, where I take the pleasure of exhibit remarkable collection of shells."

But now the Skipper raised his head, and became in a moment keenly alert; for a new figure was seen making its slow way to the wharf,—a new figure, and a singular one.

An old man, white-haired and wizen, with a face like a knife-blade, and red, blinking eyes. The face wore a look of eager yet doleful anticipation, as of a man going to execution and possessed with an intense desire to feel the edge of the axe. His thin fingers twitched and fumbled about his pockets, his lips moved, and he shook his head from time to time. This old-gentleman was clad in nankeen trousers of ancient cut, a velvet waistcoat and a blue swallow-tail coat, all greatly too large for him. His scant locks were crowned by a cheap straw hat of the newest make, his shoes and gaiters were of a twenty-year-old pattern. Altogether, he was not an ordinary-looking old gentleman, nor was his appearance agreeable; but the village people took no special notice of him, being well used to Mr. Endymion Scraper and his little ways. They knew that he was wearing out the clothes that his extravagant uncle had left behind him at his death, twenty years ago. They had seen three velvet waistcoats worn out, and one of brocade; there were sixteen left, as any woman in the village could tell you. As for the nankeen trousers, some people said there were ten dozen of them in the great oak chest, but that might be an exaggeration.

Walking just behind this pleasant old person, with feet that tried to go sedately, and not betray by hopping and skippings the joy that was in them, came the boy John; brought along in case there should be a parcel to carry. Mr. Scraper had brought, too, his supple bamboo cane, in case of need; it was a cane of singular parts, and had a way that was all its own of curling about the legs and coming up " rap " against the tender part of the calf. The boy John was intimately acquainted with the cane; therefore, when his legs refused to go steadily, but danced in spite of him, he had dropped behind Mr. Endymion, and kept well out of reach of the searching snake of polished cane.

The Skipper greeted the new-comer with his loftiest courtesy, which was quite thrown away on the old gentleman.

"Hey! hey!" said Mr. Scraper, nodding his head, and fumbling in his waistcoat pocket, "got some shells, I hear! Got some shells, eh? Nothing but rubbish, I'll swear; nothing but rubbish. Seen 'em all before you were born; not worth looking at, I'll bet a pumpkin."

"Why, Deacon Scraper, how you do talk!" exclaimed pretty Lena Brown, who was standing near by. "The shells are just elegant, I think; too handsome for anything."

"All rubbish! all rubbish!" the old gentleman repeated, hastily. "Children's nonsense, every bit of it. Have you got anything out of the common, though? have you, hey?"

He looked up suddenly at the Skipper, screwing his little eyes at him like animated corkscrews; but he read nothing in the large, calm gaze that met his.

" The gentleman please to step down in the cabin," the Skipper said, with a stately gesture. "At liberty in a moment, I shall take the pleasure to exhibit my collection. The gentleman is a collector?" he added, quietly; but this Mr. Scraper would not hear of.

"Nothing of the sort!" he cried, testily, "nothing of the sort! Just came down here with this fool boy, to keep him from falling into the water. Don't know one shell from another when I see 'em."

This astounding statement brought a low cry from John, who had been standing on one foot with joy and on the other with fear, the grave dignity of his new friend filling him with awe. Perhaps he would not be noticed now, when all the grown people were here; perhaps — but his thoughts were put to flight by Mr. Scraper's words. John was a truthful boy, and he could not have the Spanish man think he had lied in saying that the old man was a collector. He was stepping forward, his face alight with eager protest, when Mr. Endymion Scraper brought his cane round with a backward sweep, catching John on the legs with spiteful emphasis. The Skipper saw it, and a dark red flushed through the bronze of his cheek. His glance caught the child's and held it, speaking anger, cheer, and the promise of better things; the boy dropped back and rubbed his smarting shins, well content, with a warm feeling about the heart.

"The gentleman will step down to the cabin," said the deep, quiet voice. "I will attend him, the ladies also."

He led the way, and pretty Lena Brown came next; she glanced up at him as he held out his strong hand to help her down the ladder. Her blue eyes were very sweet as she met his gaze, and the faint wild-rose blush became her well. Certainly, Lena was a very pretty girl. Franci nearly tumbled over the companion-rail in his endeavours to look after her, and Laurentus Woodcock, catching one glimpse of her face, retreated to the farthest corner of the after-deck, and sold a Triton for ten cents, when the lowest price was thirty.

Several other persons came down into the cabin at the same time. There was Mr. Bill Hen Pike. Mr. Bill Hen had been a sailor himself fifty years ago, and it was a point of honour with him to visit anything with keel and sails that came up the river. He used nautical expressions whenever it could be managed, and was the village authority on all sea-going matters.

There were Isaac Cutter and his wife, who had money to spend, and were not averse to showing it; there was Miss Eliza Clinch, who had spent her fifty years of life in looking for a bargain, which she had not yet found; and some others. But though the Skipper was courteous to all, he kept close to the side of Mr. Endymion Scraper; and the boy John, and Lena Brown, who was always kind to him, kept close beside the other two. The girl was enchanted with what she saw, but her joy was chiefly in the trinkets that filled the glass counter, — the necklaces and bracelets, the shell hairpins and mother-of-pearl porte-monnaies.

" Aint they handsome ? " she cried, over and over, surveying the treasures with clasped hands and shining eyes. " Oh, Johnny ! isn't that just elegant ? Did you ever see such beautiful things ? I don't think the President's wife has no handsomer than them ! "

John frowned a little at these ecstasies, and glanced at the Skipper ; but the Skipper was apparently absorbed in polishing the Royal Tritons, and showing them to Mr. Scraper, who regarded them with disdainful eyes, while his fingers twitched to lay hold of them.

" Why, Lena, you don't want to be looking at those things ! " the boy urged. " See ! here are the shells ! Here are the real ones, not made up into truck, but just themselves. Oh, oh ! Lena, look ! "

The Skipper was coming forward with a shell in his hand of exquisite colour and shape.

" Perhaps the young lady like to see this ? " he said. " This the Voluta Musica, — a valuable shell, young lady. You look, and see the lines of the staff on the shell, so ? Here they run, you see ! The mermaids under the water, they have among themselves no sheet-music, so on shells they must read it. Can the young lady follow the notes if she take the shell in her hand ? "

He laid the lovely thing in the girl's hand, and marked how the polished lip and the soft pink palm wore the same tender shade of rose; but he said nothing of this, for he was not Franci.

Lena examined the shell curiously. "It does look like music!" she said. "But there ain't really any notes, are there? Not like our notes, I mean. If there was, I should admire to see how they sounded on the reed organ. It would make a pretty pin, if 't was n't so big!"

She was about to hand the shell back quietly — she looked like a rose-leaf in moonlight, this pretty Lena, but she was practical, and had little imagination — but John caught it from her with a swift yet timorous motion.

"I want to hear it," he said, his pleading eyes on the Skipper's face. "I want to hear what it says!"

The dark man nodded and smiled; but a moment later, seeing the lean fingers of Mr. Endymion Scraper about to clutch the treasure, he took it quietly in his own hand again, and turned to the old man.

"Gentleman spoke to me?" he inquired, blandly.

The gentleman had not spoken, but had made a series of gasps and grunts, expressive of extreme impatience and eagerness.

"That's a poor specimen," he cried now, eying the shell greedily, "a very poor specimen! What do you expect to get for it, hey?"

"A perfect specimen!" replied the Skipper, calmly. "The gentleman has but to look at it closer" — and he held it nearer to the greedy corkscrew eyes — "to see that it is a rare specimen, more perfect than often seen in museums. I brought up this shell myself, with care choosing it; its price is five dollars."

Mr. Endymion Scraper gave a scream, which he tried to turn into a disdainful chuckle.

"Five cents would be nearer it!" he cried, angrily. "Think we're all fools down here, hey? Go 'long with your five dollars."

"No, Señor, not all fools!" said the Skipper. "Many varieties among men, as among shells. I am in no haste to sell the Voluta Musica. It has its price, as gentleman knows by his catalogue. Here is a razor-shell; perhaps the gentleman like that. Shave yourself or other people with this!"

"I want to know!" interposed Mrs. Isaac Cutter, leaning forward eagerly, spectacles on nose. "Can folks really shave with those, sir? They do look sharp, now, don't they? What might you ask for a pair?"

"Perhaps not very easy to grind, lady!" replied the Skipper, with a smile which won Mrs. Isaac's heart. "Not a rare shell, only fifty cents the pair. Thank you, madam! To show you this? With gladness! This is the Bleeding Tooth shell, found in plenty in West Indies. They have also dentists under the sea, graciously observe. See here,—the whole family! The baby, he have as yet no tooth, the little gum smooth and white. Here, the boy! (*Como ti*, Juan Colorado!" this in a swift aside, caught only by John's ear.) "The boy, he have a tooth pulled, you observe, madam; here the empty space, with blood-mark, thus. Hence the name, Bleeding Tooth. Here the father, getting old, has lost two teeth, bleeding much; and this being the old grandfather, all teeth are gone, again. Yes, curious family! You kindly accept these persons, madam, with a wish that you never suffer of this manner."

Mrs. Isaac Cutter drew a long breath, and took the shells with a look of delighted awe. "Well, I'm sure!" she said, "you're more than kind, sir. I never thought — I do declare — Bleeding Tooth! Well, father, if that isn't something to tell the folks at home!" Mr. Isaac Cutter grunted, well pleased, and said, "That so!" several times, his vocabulary being limited.

"Again, here," the Skipper continued, with a glance around, to make sure that his audience was attentive, "again, here a curious thing, ladies and gentlemen. The Nighthawk shell, not common in any part of the world. The two halves held together of this manner, behold the nighthawk, as he flies through the air!"

A murmur of delight ran through the little group, and Mr. Endymion Scraper edged to the front, his fingers twitching convulsively.

"How much — how much do you want for that Night-hawk?" he asked, stammering with eagerness. "'Taint wuth much, but — what — ten dollars? I'll give ye three, and not a cent more."

But the Skipper put him aside with a wave of his hand.

"Another time, sir," he said; "at future interview I will make arrangements with you, and hope to satisfy; at present I instruct these ladies a little in life under the sea.

"Lady," he said, and it was observable that although he spoke to Mrs. Isaac Cutter, his eyes rested on Lena, and on the boy John, who stood behind her, " Nature of her abundance is very generous to the sea. Here all fishes swim, great and small; but more! All things that on earth find their place, of them you find a picture, copy, what you please to call it, at the bottom of the sea. A few only are yet found by men, yet strange things also have I seen. Not under the ocean do you think to find violets growing, is it so? yet here you observe a handful of violets, in colour as on a green bank, though without perfume, the sunshine wanting in those places."

He drew from a box some of the exquisite little violet snail-shells, and gave them to Lena, who cried out with delight, and instantly resolved to have a pair of ear-rings made of them.

" The ladies are hungry?" the quiet voice went on. " They desire breakfast? I offer them a poached egg, grown under the sea. The colour and shape perfect; the water ladies eat them every morning, but with the air they grow hard and lose their flavour. Thank you, madam! for thirty cents only, the poached egg, not a rare variety. Your smile perhaps will make it soft again. I hope you enjoy it at luncheon.

" But before luncheon you desire to prepare your charming toilet? Here I offer you a comb, ladies, as they use under the sea. The story, that Venus, goddess of beauty, when she rose from the ocean, dropped from her hand the comb with which she arranged even then her locks of gold: hence the name, Venus's Comb. Observe the long teeth, necessary for fine hair, like that of Venus and these ladies."

Mrs. Isaac Cutter bridled, smoothed her " fluffy Fedora " (price one dollar and fifty cents, ready curled), and bought the " comb " on the spot.

" Of little boys under the sea," the Skipper continued, — and once more his smile fell on the boy John, and produced that agreeable sensation of warmth about the heart to which the little fellow had been long unaccustomed, — " there are many. They swim about, they play, they sport, they go to school, as little boys here. They ride, some persons have told me, on the horse-mackerel, but of that I have no knowledge. I see for myself, however, that they play tops, the small sea-boys. Here, little gentleman, is the Imperial Top, — very beautiful shell. You like to take it in your hand ? "

John took the splendid thing, and straightway lost himself and the world in a dream of rapture, in which he descended to the depths that his soul desired, and played at spinning tops with the sea-boys, and rode a horse-mackerel, and did many other wonderful things.

" The bat shell!" the Skipper went on, lifting one treasure and then another. " The Voluta Aulica, extremely rare, — the Mitres, worn by bishops under the sea. The bishops must be chosen very small, lady, to fit the shell, since shells were made first. The Queen Conch ! This again, — pardon me, gentleman, you desire to assist me ? Too kind, but I shall not give that trouble to a visitor ! "

The last remark was addressed to Mr. Endymion Scraper, who had for the last five minutes been sidling quietly, and as he thought unobserved, toward the shelf on which lay the Voluta Musica. His claw-like fingers, after hovering over the prize, had finally closed upon it, and he was about to slip it into his pocket without more ado, when a strong brown hand descended upon his wrist. The shell was quietly taken from him, and looking up in impotent rage, he met the dark eyes of the Skipper gazing at him with cheerful gravity.

"Price five dollars!" he murmured, courteously. "In a box, gentleman? But, certainly! A valuable specimen. Thank you kindly. Five-dollar bill, quite right! Exhibition is over for this morning, ladies and gentlemen, to resume in afternoon hours, if graciously pleased to honour the shell schooner,—schooner 'Nautilus,' from the Bahamas, with remarkable collection of marine curiosities."

CHAPTER IV.

ABOARD THE "NAUTILUS."

THE shell schooner had many visitors during the next few days, as she lay by the wharf; visitors, of whom a few came to buy, but by far the greater part to look and gossip, and see the monkeys, and ask questions. The monkeys, Jack and Jim, were no small part of the attraction, being delightful little beasts, bright of eye and friendly of heart, always ready to turn a somersault, or to run up the mast, or to make a bow to the ladies (always with Franci in their hearts), as the Skipper directed them.

Of course John was there at every available minute, whenever he could escape the searching of his guardian's eye and tongue; but Mr. Scraper himself came several times to the "Nautilus;" so did pretty Lena Brown. There was no doubt that Lena was a charming girl. She looked like moonlight, Rento thought; John thought so, too, though he knew that the resemblance went no further than looks. Her hair was soft and light, with a silvery glint when the sun struck it, and it had a pretty trick of falling down about her forehead in two Madonna-like bands, framing the soft, rose-tinted cheeks sweetly enough, and hiding with the pale shining tresses the narrowness of the white forehead.

Lena was apt to come with John, to whom she was

always kind, though she thought him "cracked," and after a little desultory hovering about the shells, for which she did not really care, except when they were made up with glass beads, she was apt to sit down on the after-deck, with John beside her (unless the Skipper appeared, in which case the boy flew to join his new friend), and with Franci, or Rento, or both, sure to be near by. The monkeys never failed to come and nestle down beside the boy, and examine his pockets and chatter confidentially in his ear; and John always nodded and seemed to understand, which Lena considered foolishness. She thought she came out of pure kindness for the boy, because " that old gimlet never would let him come alone, and the child was fairly possessed about the shells;" but it is to be doubted whether she would have come so often if it had not been for Franci's admiring glances and Rento's deeper veneration, which seldom dared to look higher than the hem of her gown.

She would sit very demurely on the after-deck, apparently absorbed in the shells and corals that lay spread before her; and by-and-by, it might be, Franci, who did not suffer from shyness, would venture on something more definite than admiring glances.

He would show her the shells, making the most of his knowledge, which was not extensive, and calling in invention when information failed; but he liked better to talk of himself, Franci, and on that subject there was plenty to be said. He was a prince, he told Lena, in South America, where he came from. This was a poor country, miserable country; but in his own the houses were all of marble, pink marble, with mahogany door-steps.

" Is that so ? " Lena would say, raising her limpid eyes to the dark velvety ones that were bent so softly on her.

" Oh, fine! fine! " said Franci. " Never I eat from a china dish in my country; silver, all silver! Only the pigs eat from china. Drink wine, eat peaches and ice-cream all days, all time. My sister wear gold clothes, trimmed diamonds, when she do her washing. Yes! Like to go there ? " and he bent over Lena with an enchanting smile.

" Why do you tell such lies ? " asked John, whom Franci had not observed, as he was lying in one of the schooner's boats, with a monkey on either arm. Franci's smile deepened as he turned toward the boy, swearing softly in Spanish, and feeling in his breast; but at that momont Rento happened to stroll that way, blushing deeply at Lena's nearness, yet with a warlike expression in his bright blue eyes. Franci told him he was the son of a pig that had died of the plague, and that he, Franci, devoutly hoped the son would share the fate of his mother, without time to consult a priest. Rento replied that he could jaw as much as he was a mind to, so long as he let the boy alone; and Lena looked from one to the other with a flush on her pretty cheek, and an instinct that made her heart beat a little faster.

Mr. Scraper's visits were apt to be made in the evening; his passion for shells was like that for drink, and he would fain have hidden it from the eyes of his neighbours.

It was always a trial to Franci to know that the old miser, as he called Mr. Endymion, was in the cabin, and that he, Franci, must keep watch on deck while this withered anatomy sat on the cabin chairs and drank with the Patron. Franci's way of keeping watch was to lie at full length on the deck with his feet in the air, smoking cigarettes. It was not the regulation way, but Franci did not care for that. That beast of a Rento was asleep, snoring like a pig that he was, while his betters must keep awake and gaze at this desolating prospect; the Patron was in the cabin with the miser, and no one thought of the individual who alone gave charm to the schooner. He, Franci, would make himself as comfortable as might be, and would not care a puff of his cigar if the schooner and all that were in it, except himself, should go to the bottom the next minute. No! Rather would he dance for joy, and wave his hand, and cry, " Good voyage, Patron! Good voyage, brute of a pig-faced Rento! Good voyage, old ' Nautilus! ' Go all to the bottom with my blessing, and I dance on the wharf, and marry the pretty Lena, and get all the old miser's money, and wear velvet coats. Ah! Franci, my handsome little boy, why did you let them send you to sea, hearts of stone that they were! You, born to shine, to adorn, to break the hearts of maidens! Why? tell me that!" He waved his legs in the air, and contemplated with delight their proportions, which were certainly exquisite. " Caramba!" he murmured; "beauty, that is it! Otherwise one might better be a swine,—yes, truly!"

At this point, perhaps, Rento appeared, rubbing his eyes,

evidently just awake, and ready to take his watch; where-
upon the beautiful one sat up, and, fixing his eyes on his
fellow - seaman, executed a series of grimaces which did
great credit to his invention and power of facial expression.   Then he delivered himself of an harangue in purest
Spanish, to the effect that the day was not far distant when
he, Franci, would slit Rento's nose with a knife, and carve
his initials on his cheeks, and finally run him through the
so detestable body and give him to the fish to devour,
though with strong fears of his disagreeing with them.   To
which Rento replied that he might try it just as soon as he
was a mind to, but that at this present moment he was to
get out; which the beautiful youth accordingly did, retir-
ing with a dancing step, expressive of scorn and disgust.

On one such night as this the scene in the little cabin
was a curious one.   A lamp burned brightly on the table,
and its lights shone on a number of objects, some lying
openly on the green table-cover, some reclining superbly in
velvet-lined cases.   Shells!   Yes, but not such shells as
were heaped in profusion on shelf and counter.   Those
were lovely, indeed, and some of them of considerable value;
but it was a fortune, no less, that lay now spread before
the eyes of the Skipper and his guest.   For these were
the days when fine shells could not be bought on every
hand, as they can to-day; when a good specimen of the
Imperial Harp brought two hundred and fifty dollars
easily, and when a collector would give anything, even to
the half of his kingdom (if he were a collector of the right
sort), for a Precious Wentletrap.

It was a Wentletrap on which the little red eyes of Mr.
Endymion Scraper were fixed at this moment. The
morocco case in which it lay was lined with crimson
velvet, and the wonderful shell shone purely white against
the glowing colour, — snow upon ice; for the body of the
shell was semi-transparent, the denser substance of the
spiral whorls turning them to heavy snow against the
shining clearness beneath them. Has any of my readers
seen a Precious Wentletrap? Then he knows one of the
most beautiful things that God has made.

Apparently the Skipper had just opened the case, for Mr.
Scraper was sitting with his mouth wide open, staring at it
with greedy, almost frightened eyes. Truly, a perfect
specimen of this shell was, in those days, a thing seen only
in kings' cabinets; yet no flaw appeared in this, no blot
upon its perfect beauty. The old miser sat and stared,
and only his hands, which clutched the table-cloth in a convulsive grasp, and his greedy eyes, showed that he was not
turned to stone. He had been amazed enough by the
other treasures, as the Skipper had taken them one by one
from the iron safe in the corner, whose door now hung
idly open. Where had been seen such Pheasants as these,
— the fragile, the exquisite, the rarely perfect? Even the
Australian Pheasant, rarest of all, lay here before him,
with its marvellous pencillings of rose and carmine and
gray. Mr. Endymion's mouth had watered at the mere
description of the shell in the catalogue, but he had never
thought to see one, except the imperfect specimen in the
museum at Havenborough. Here, too, was the Orange

Cowry; here the Bishop's Mitre, and the precious Voluta Aulica; while yonder,— what was this man, that he should have a Voluta Junonia, of which only a few specimens are possessed in the known world? What did it all mean?

The Skipper sat beside the table, quiet and self-contained as usual. His arm lay on the table, his hand was never far from the more precious shells, and his eyes did not leave the old man's face; but he showed no sign of uneasiness. Why should he, when he could have lifted Mr. Endymion with his left hand and set him at any minute at the top of the cabin stairs? Now and then he took up a shell with apparent carelessness (though in reality he handled them with fingers as fine as a woman's, knowing their every tenderest part, and where they might best be approached without offence to their delicacy), looked it over, and made some remark about its quality or value; but for the most part he was silent, letting the shells speak for themselves and make their own effect.

The old man had been wheezing and grunting painfully for some minutes, opening and shutting his hands, and actually scratching the table-cloth in his distress. At length he broke out, after a long silence.

"Who are ye, I want to know? How come you by these shells? I know something about what they're wuth — that is — well, I know they aint wuth what you say they are, well enough; but they air wuth a good deal, — I know that. What I want to understand is, what you're after here! What do you want, and why do you show me these things if — if — you come by them honestly. Hey?"

The Skipper smiled meditatively. " Yes ! " he said,
" we all like to know things, — part of our nature, sir —
part of our nature. I, now, I like to know things, too.
What you going to do with that boy, Mr. Scrape? I like
to know that. You tell me, and perhaps you hear something about the shells, who know ? "

The old man's face darkened into a very ugly look.

" My name is Scraper, thank ye, not Scrape ! " he said,
dryly ; " and as for the boy, I don't know exactly where
you come in there."

The Skipper nodded. "True ! " he said, tracing with
his finger the fine lines of the Voluta Aulica ; " you do not
know where I come in there. In us both, knowledge has
a limit, Mr. Scraper ; yet I at the least am acquaint with
your name. It is a fine name you have there, — Endymion !
You should be a person of poetry, with this and your love
for shells, hein ? You love, without doubt, to gaze on the
moon, Sir Scraper ? You feel with her a connection, yes ? "

" What the dickens are you talking about ? " asked the
old gentleman, testily. " How much do you want to swin-
dle me out of for this Junonia, hey ? not that I shall buy
it, mind ye ! "

" Three hundred ! " said the Skipper ; " and a bargain at
that ! "

CHAPTER V.

MYSTERY.

JOHN was at work in the garden. At least, so it would have appeared to an ordinary observer; in reality he was carrying on a sanguinary combat, and dealing death on every side. His name was George Washington, and he was at Bunker Hill (where he certainly had no business to be), and the British were intrenched behind the cabbages. "They 've just got down into the ground, they are so frightened!" he said to himself, pausing to straighten his aching back, and toss the red curls out of his eyes. "See 'em, all scrooched down, with their feet in the earth, trying to make believe they grow there! But I 'll have 'em out! Whack! there goes the general. Come out, I say !" He wrestled fiercely with an enormous Britisher, disguised as a stalk of pig-weed, and, after a breathless tussle, dragged him bodily out of the ground, and flung his headless corpse on the neighbouring pile of weeds.

"Ha! that was fine !" cried the boy. "I should n't be a bit surprised if that was George the Third himself; it was ugly enough for him. Come up here! hi! down with you! Now Jack the Giant-Killer is coming to help me, and the British have got Cormoran (this was before Jack killed him), and there 's going to be a terrible row." But

General Washington waves his gallant sword, and calls to his men, and says, —

" Good morning, sir! you make a busy day, I see."

It was not General Washington who spoke. It was the Skipper, and he was leaning on the gate and looking at the boy John and smiling. "You make a busy day," he repeated. " I think there are soon no more weeds in Sir Scraper's garden."

" Oh, yes!" cried John, straightening himself again, and leaning on his trusty hoe. "There'll be just as many — I beg your pardon! Good morning! I hope you are well; it is a very fine day. There'll be just as many of them to-morrow, or next day, certainly. I make believe they are the British, you see, and I've been fighting all the morning, and I do think they are pretty well licked by this time; but they don't stay licked, the British don't. I like them for that, don't you? Even though it is a bother to go on fighting all the days of one's life."

" I also have noticed that of the British!" the Skipper said, nodding gravely. " But now you can rest a little, Juan Colorado? Sir Scraper is at home, that you call him for me, say I desire to make him the visit?"

" No, he is n't at home," said John. " He's gone down to the store for his mail. But please come in and wait, and he'll be back soon. Do come in! It — it's cool to rest, after walking in the sun."

It was the only inducement the child could think of, but he offered it with right good-will. The Skipper assented with a smile and a nod, and the two passed into the house together.

In the kitchen, which was the living-room of the house, John halted, and brought a chair for his visitor, and prepared to play the host as well as he could ; but the visitor seemed, for some reason, not to fancy the kitchen. He looked around with keen, searching eyes, scanning every nook and corner in the bare little room. Truly, there was not much to see. The old fireplace had been blocked up, and in its place was the usual iron cooking-stove, with a meagre array of pots and pans hanging behind it. The floor was bare ; the furniture, a table and chair, with a stool for John. There was no provision for guests; but that did not matter, as Mr. Scraper never had guests. Altogether, there was little attraction in the kitchen, and the Skipper seemed curiously displeased with its aspect.

"There is no other room ?" he asked, after completing his survey. " No better room than this, Colorado ? Surely, there must be one other ; yes, of course !" he added, as if struck by a sudden thought. " His shells ? Mr. Scraper has shells. They are — where ? "

He paused and looked sharply at the boy. Little John coloured high. " The — the shells ?" he stammered. " Yes, of course, sir, the shells are in another room, in the parlour; but — but — I am not let go in there, unless Mr. Scraper sends me."

" So !" said the dark man; " but for me, Colorado, how is it for me ? Mr. Scraper never said to me that I must not go in this parlour, you see. For you it is well, you do as you are told ; you are a boy that makes himself to trust ; for me, I am a Skipper from the Bahamas, I do some things that are strange to you,—among them, this. I go into the parlour."

He nodded lightly, and leaving the child open-mouthed in amazement, opened the sacred door, the door of the best parlour, and went in, as unconcernedly as if it were his own cabin. John, standing at the door,— he surely might go as far as the door, if he did not step over the threshold,— watched him, and his eyes grew wider and wider, and his breath came quicker and quicker.

For the Skipper was doing strange things, as he had threatened. Advancing quickly into the middle of the room, he cast around him the same searching glance with which he had scanned the kitchen. He went to the window, and threw back the blinds. The sunlight streamed in, as if it, too, were eager to see what shrouded treasures were kept secluded here. Probably the blinds had not been thrown back since Gran'ther Scraper died.

The parlour was scarcely less grim than the kitchen, though there was a difference in its grimness. Seven chairs stood against the wall, like seven policemen with their hands behind their backs; a table crouched in the middle, its legs bent as if to spring. The boy John considered the table a monster, transformed by magic into its present shape, and likely to be released at any moment, and to leap at the unwary intruder. Its faded cover, with two ancient ink-blots which answered for eyes, fostered this idea, which was a disquieting one. On the wall hung two silver coffin-plates in a glass case, testifying that Freeborn Scraper, and Elmira his wife, had been duly buried, and that their

coffins had presented a good appearance at the funeral.
But the glory of the room, in the boy John's eyes, was the
cabinet of shells which stood against the opposite wall.
He had once thought this the chief ornament of the
world; he knew better now, but still he regarded its
treasures with awe and veneration, and looked to see the
expression of delight which should overspread the features
of his new friend at sight of it. What, then, was his
amazement to see his new friend pass over the cabinet
with a careless glance, as if it were the most ordinary
thing in the world! Evidently, it was not shells that he
had come to see; and the boy grew more and more mysti-
fied. Suddenly the dark eyes lightened; the whole face
flashed into keen attention. What had the Skipper seen?
Nothing, apparently, but the cupboard in the corner, the
old cupboard where Mr. Scraper kept his medicines. The
old man had sent John to this cupboard once, when he
himself was crippled with rheumatism, to fetch him a bottle
of the favourite remedy of the day. John remembered its
inward aspect, with rows of dusty bottles, and on the upper
shelf, rows of still more dusty papers. What could the
Skipper see to interest him in the corner cupboard? Something, certainly! For now he was opening the cupboard,
quietly, as if he knew all about it and was looking for
something that he knew to be there.

"Ah!" said the Skipper; and he drew a long breath, as
of relief. " True, the words! In the corner of the parlour,
a cupboard of three corners, with bottles filled, and over
the bottles, papers. Behold the cupboard, the bottles, the

papers! A day of fortunes!" He bent forward, and proceeded to rummage in the depths of the cupboard ; but this was too much for John's conscience. " I beg your pardon, sir!" he said, timidly. " But — do you think you ought to do that?"

The Skipper looked out of the cupboard for an instant, and his eyes were very bright. " Yes, Colorado," he said. " 1 think 1 ought to do this! Oh, very much indeed, my friend, I ought to do this! And here," — he stepped back, holding something in his hand, — " here, it is done! No more disturbance, Colorado; I thank you for your countenance.

" Do we now make a promenade in the garden, to see your work ?

" Yet," he added, pausing and again looking around him, " but yet once more I observe. This room,"— it was strange, he did not seem to like the parlour any better than he had liked the kitchen — " this room, to live in! a young person, figure it, Colorado ! gentle, with desires, with dreams of beauty, and this only to behold! For companion an ancient onion, — I say things that are improper, my son! I demand pardon! But for a young person, a maiden to live here, would be sad indeed, do you think it?"

John pondered, in wonder and some trouble of mind. There was something that he had to say, something very hard ; but it would not be polite just now, and he must answer a question when he was asked. " I — I thought it was a fine room!" he said at length, timidly. " It isn't as bright, somehow, as where I used to live with my mother,

and — it seems to stay shut up, even when it is n't; but —
I guess it 's a fine room, sir ; and then, if a person did n't
like it, there 's all out-doors, you know, and that 's never
shut up."

" True ! " cried the Skipper, with a merry laugh ; " out
of doors is never shut up, praise be to Heaven ! " He
pulled off his cap, and looked up at the shining sky. They
were standing on the door-step now, and John noticed that
his companion seemed much less grave than usual. He
laughed, he patted the boy on the shoulder, he hummed
snatches of strange, sweet melodies. Once or twice he
broke out into speech, but it was foreign speech, and John
knew nothing save that it was something cheerful. They
walked about the garden, and the Skipper surveyed John's
work, and pronounced it prodigious. He questioned the
child closely, too, as to how he lived, and what he did, and
why he stayed with Mr. Scraper. But the child could tell
him little. He supposed it was all right ; his mother was
dead, and there was nobody else, and Mr. Scraper said he
was his father's uncle, and that the latter had appointed
him guardian over John in case of the mother's death.
That was all, he guessed.

" All, my faith ! " cried the Skipper, gayly. " Enough,
too, Colorado ! quite enough, in the opinion of me. But I
go, my son ! Till a little while ; you will come to-day to
the ' Nautilus,' yes ? "

But little John stood still in the path, and looked up in
his friend's face. The time had come when he must do the
hard thing, and it was harder even than he had thought it

would be. His throat was very dry, and he tried once or twice before the words would come. At last — "I beg your pardon!" he said. "I am only a little boy, and perhaps there is something I don't understand; but — but — I don't think you ought to have done that!"

"Done what, son of mine?" asked the Skipper, gazing down at him with the bright, kind eyes that he loved, and that would not be kind the next moment, perhaps. "What is it I have done?"

"To take the papers!" said John; and now his voice was steady, and he knew quite well what he must say, if only his heart would not beat so loud in his ears! "I don't think it was right; but perhaps you know things that make it right for you. But — but Mr. Scraper left me here, to take care of the house, and — and I shall have to tell him that you went into the parlour and took things out of the cupboard."

There was silence for a moment,—silence, all but the throbbing that seemed as if it must deafen the child, as it was choking him. He stood looking at the ground, his face in a flame, his eyes full of hot, smarting tears. Was it he who had stolen the papers? Surely anyone would have thought so who saw his anguish of confusion. And the Skipper did not speak! And this was his friend, the first heart-friend the child had ever had, perhaps the only one that would ever come to him, and he was affronting him, casting him off, accusing him of vileness! Unable to bear the pain any longer, the child looked up at last, and as he did so, the tears overflowed and ran down his round checks. The dark eyes were as kind as ever. They were smiling, oh, so tenderly! John hid his face on his blue sleeve, and sobbed to his heart's content; somehow, without a word, the dreadful pain was gone, and the blessed feeling had returned that this friend knew all about things, and understood little boys, and liked them.

The Skipper did not speak for a moment, only stood and stroked the boy's curly hair with a light, soft touch, almost as his mother used to stroke it. Then he said, in his deep, grave voice, that was sweeter than music, John thought,—

" Colorado! my little son, my friend!" That was enough for a few minutes, till the sobs were quieted, and only the little breast heaved and sank, tremulously, like the breast of a frightened bird. Then the Skipper led him to a rustic bench, and sat down beside him, and took his hand.

"And that hurt you to say, my little son?" he said, smiling. " That hurt you, because you thought it would vex the friend from the Bahamas, the friend who steals. And yet you like him a little, is it not?"

" Oh!" cried John, looking up with all his heart in his blue eyes; and no other word was needed.

" See, then!" the Skipper went on, still holding the boy's hand; " it is that you are right, Colorado, oh, very right, my son! and I, who am old, but old enough to be twice to you a father, I thought not of this. Yes, you must tell Sir Scraper, if — if I do not tell him first." He was silent a moment, thinking; and then continued, speaking slowly, choosing his words with care: " Is it that you think, Colorado, it would be wrong to wait a little before you tell Sir Scraper — if I said, till to-morrow? If I ask you to wait, and then, if I have not told him, you shall tell him, — what do you say of that, my son?"

John looked helplessly around, his blue eyes growing big and wistful again. "If — if he should ask me!" he said. "I am sure you know all about it, and that it is all right for you, but if he should ask me — you see — I — I should have to answer him, should n't I?"

"You would have to answer him!" the Skipper repeated, frowning thoughtfully. "And you could not tell him that there were flying-fish in the cabin, eh, Colorado? Wait then, that your friend thinks. The mind moves at times slowly, my son, slowly!"

He was silent, and John watched him, breathless.

Presently, "Will you come with me, Colorado?" asked the Skipper. "I invite you to come, to spend the day on the 'Nautilus,' to play with Jack and Jim, to polish the shells, — what you please. I desire not longer to wait here, I desire not that yet Sir Scraper know of my visit. Had he been here, other happenings might have been; as it is — shortly, will you come with me, Colorado?"

John shut his eyes tight, and took possession of his soul.

"I promised!" he said, "I promised him that if he would not whip me this morning I would not stir off the place. He was mad because I went yesterday, and he was going to give me a good one this morning, and I had n't got over the last good one, and so — I promised that! But if I had known you were coming," he cried, "I would not have promised, and I would have taken three good ones, if I could only go."

The Skipper nodded, and was silent again. Suddenly he rose to his feet.

"Have you heard of pirates, Colorado?" he asked, abruptly.

John nodded, wondering.

"Of Malay pirates?" the Skipper continued, with animation. "They are wild fellows, those! They come, they see a person, they carry him off, to keep at their fancy, till a ransom is paid, or till he grow old and die, or till they kill him the next day, who knows? But not all are bad fellows, and there are some of them who are kind to captives, who take them on board their ships, play with them, show to them strange things, shells and fish and corals, all things. Have you ever played at pirate, Colorado?"

"Yes, sometimes," the boy admitted, wondering still more at the brightness in his friend's look, and his air of sudden determination.

"I never played Malay, only Portugee; I thought they were n't so cruel, but I don't know. I had a ship down by the wharf, and I made a good many pirate voyages round the wharf, and sometimes quite a piece down river, when I could get the time. But then, after a while, I thought it was nicer to be a rescuing ship, and get folks away from the pirates, you know, so I 've done that lately, and I 've rescued as many as twenty vessels, I should think."

"That was fine!" said the Skipper, nodding sagely. "That was well done, Colorado! But here we come to

trouble, do you see? for I that speak to you — I am a
Malay pirate!"

The boy started violently and looked up, expecting he
knew not what sudden and awful change in the face that
bent down over him; but no! it was the same quiet, dark
face, only there was a bright gleam in the eyes. A
gleam of fun, was it? Surely not of ferocity.

"I come up this river," the Skipper continued, rapidly,
" to see what I find, — perhaps gold, perhaps silver, perhaps
prisoners of value. I look about, I see the pleasant village, I see persons very amiable, but no precious thing
except one; that one, I have it! I am a Malay pirate,
Colorado, and thus I carry off my prize!" and picking up
the child as if he were a feather, and tossing him up to
his shoulder, the Skipper strode from the garden, and took
his way toward the wharf.

CHAPTER VI.

MR. BILL HEN.

MR. BILL HEN PIKE had come to have a good long gossip. It was some time since a schooner had come up the river, for the ice-shipping had not yet begun, and he was fairly thirsting for maritime intelligence. He desired to know the tonnage of the "Nautilus," her age, where she was built, and by whom; her original cost, and what sums had been expended in repairs since she had been in the Skipper's possession; how many trips she had made, to what ports, and with what cargoes; the weather that had been encountered on each and every trip. These things and many more of like import did the Skipper unfold, sitting at ease on the cabin table, while Mr. Bill Hen tilted the only chair in rhythmic content. His hat was tilted, too; his broad red face shone with pleasure; the world was a good place to him, full of information.

At last the questions came to an end; it seemed a pity, but there was really nothing left to ask, since it appeared that the Skipper was unmarried and had no relations. But now the Skipper's own turn had come, and quietly, with just enough show of interest to be polite, he began the return game. "You have been at sea a large part of your life, Señor Pike?"

"Oh, yes! yes! I'm well used to the sea. That is —

off and on, you know, off and on. I was mate on a coasting schooner, saw a good deal that way, you know; like the sea first-rate, but my wife, she won't hear to my going off nowadays, and there 's the farm to ' tend to, stock and hay, var'ous things, var'ous things; all about it, my sea-going days are over, yes, yes! Pleasant place, though, pleasant place, though the strength going out of my legs makes it troublesome by times, yes, yes! Been in these parts before, you said ? Oh, no ! said you had n't ; beg your pardon ! Pleasant part of the country ! good soil, good neighbours."

"Fine country, I should suppose!" said the Skipper; "and as you say, sir, the persons agreeable for knowledge. You know the boy whom I hear called John, with the old gentleman who collects shells?"

"Oh! ho!" said Mr. Bill Hen, delighted to find a fresh subject of interest. "Deacon Scraper, yes, yes! well named, sir, Deacon Scraper is, well named, you see! Very close man, pizeon close they do say. Lived here all his life, Deacon Scraper has, and made a fortune. Scraped it, some say, out of folks as weren't so well off as he, but I don't know. Keen after shells, the old gentleman, yes, yes! like liquor to him, I 've heard say. Never a man to drink or what you might call royster, no way of the world but just that; but get him off to Boston, or any place where there were shells to be bought, and he 'd come home fairly drunk with 'em, his trunk busting out and all his money gone. Seems cur'ous, too, for such an old rip as Dym Scraper, *to* care for such things ; but we 're made sing'lar,— one one way, and 'nother one t' other. That's so, I reckon, in your part of the world as well as hereabouts ?"

The Skipper bowed his head gravely. "The nature of humans is without doubt the same in many lands," he said. "The little boy whom I hear called John, — he is of near blood to this old gentleman, yes ?"

But here Mr. Bill Hen grew redder in the face, which was a difficult feat, and smote the cabin table.

"Burning shame it is about that youngster!" he declared. "Burning shame, if ever there was one in this mortal world. How some folks can set by and see things going on *as* they 're going on, beats me, and le' me say I 'm hard to beat. That child, sir, is an orphan; got no father nor mother, let alone grandf'ther or grandm'ther, in the land of the living. His father was some kind of a natural, I guess, or else he had n't known Deacon Scraper by sight or hearing; but when he dies what does he do but leave that old — old — beetle-bug guardeen of that child, case of his mother dyin'. Well, if I 'd ha' had children, I might leave 'em to a fox for guardeen, or I might leave 'em to a horned pout, whichever I was a mind to, but I would n't leave 'em to Dym Scraper, and you can chalk that up on the door any ways you like." The good man paused, and puffed and snorted for some minutes in silence. The Skipper waited, his dark face quietly attentive, his eyes very bright.

"Near blood ?" Mr. Bill Hen broke out again, with another blow on the table. "No, he aint so dretful near blood, if you come to that. Near as the child 's got, though, seemin'ly. His father, Johnny's father, was son to Freeborn Scraper, the Deacon's twin brother. Twins they was, though no more alike than pork and peas. Them two, and Zenoby, the sister, who married off with a furriner and was never heerd of again; but she ain't in the story, though some say she was her father's favourite, and that Dym gave her no peace, after Freeborn left, till he got rid of her. All about it, Freeborn went West young, and spent his days there; lived comfortable, and left means when he died. Dym Scraper, he went out to the funeral, and run it, we heerd, Freeborn's wife being dead and his son weakly; anyway, he brung back them two silver coffin-plates that hangs in the parlour to his house. Next thing we knew — good while after, y' understand, but first thing *we* knew, here to the village — the son was dead, too; Mahlon his name was, and had been weakly all his days. Deacon Scraper went out agin, and kinder scraped round, folks reckoned, 'peared to make of the young widder, and meeched up to her, and all. Wal! And here this last year, if *she* does n't up and die! Sing'lar gift folks has for dying out in them parts; living so fur from the sea, I've always cal'lated. All about it, that old spider goes out the third time, and no coffin-plates this time, but he brings back the boy; and lo, ye! he's made full guardeen over the child, and has him, body and soul.

"Now I aint a malicious man, no way of the world, Mister, — well, whatever your name is. But I tell you, that old weasel is laying for something ugly about that youngster. Some say he's applied to send him to the

Reform School; good little boy as I'd want to see. I believe it's so. Don't tell me! He's got money, that child has, or land, and Dym Scraper means to have it. The child's got no one in the world to look to, and folks about here are so skeered of Deacon Scraper that they'll set by, I believe, and see a thing like that done before their eyes. I tell ye what, sir, I'm a church-member, and I don't want to say nothing but what's right and proper; but if there was a prophet anyways handy in these times (and a mighty good thing to have round, too), there'd be fire and brimstun called down on Dym Scraper, and the hull village would turn out to see him get it, too!"

"But you, sir!" said the Skipper, who had his knife out now, and was carving strange things on the table, as was his manner when moved. "You will not permit such a thing, a person of heart as you have the air to be? No, you will not permit that a thing enormous take place at your side?"

Mr. Bill Hen's face grew purple; he drew out a large handkerchief and wiped his forehead, puffing painfully; there was a pause.

"Married man?" he said, at length. "No, beg your pardon, unmarried, I remember. Well, sir, you may know something of life, but there's a sight you don't know yet. See?"

Again there was silence, the Skipper gazing darkly at his carven runes, Mr. Bill Hen still puffing and wiping his brow.

"Yes, there's a sight you don't know about," he said

again. " My wife, you see, she 's a good woman, there 's no better woman round; but she 's masterful, sir, she 's masterful, and I 'm a man who 's always led a quiet life and desire peace. And there 's more behind; though why on the airth I 'm telling you all this is more than I can tell!"

The last words came with a peevish outburst, and he hesitated, as if minded to say no more; but the Skipper raised his head, and the dark eyes sent out a compelling glance. The weaker man faltered, gave way, and resumed his speech.

" She 's a masterful woman, I tell ye! She thinks Deacon Scraper is a dangerous man, and there aint nobody here but what 'll agree with her that far. Then — he — he 's got a mortgage on my farm, same as he has on others, — plenty of others as is better clothed with means than ever I 've been; and, all about it, my wife aint willing for us to make an enemy of the old man. That 's where the land lays, and you can see for yourself. Plenty in the village is fixed the same way; he 's got power, that old grape-skin has, power over better men than he. We don't want to see that child put upon, but we aint no blood to him, and there aint anybody but feels that he himself aint just the one to interfere. That 's the way my wife feels, and I, —well, there now! you 're a stranger, and I may never set eyes on you again; but I take to you, somehow, and I don't mind telling you that I feel as mean as dirt whenever I think of that lamb in that old fox's den ; mean as dirt I feel, and yet I aint got the spunk to — the strenth is gone out of my legs," he added, piteously, " these ten years back, and I think some of my sperrit went with it. That's where it is! I haint got the sperrit to stand up against 'em."

There was a long silence, and then the Skipper shut his knife with a click, and rose from the table, holding out his hand.

"You are a good man, Señor Pike," he said. "I think no worse of you, and am glad to make the acquaintance. With regard to this child, I shall remind you,"—here he shook his head with a backward gesture in which there was something at once proud and humble, —"I shall remind you that there are powers very high, more high than of prophets; and that God will do the works as seems Him good. I may have the honour to wait upon your distinguished lady at a future day; I think to be some days in this place, for purposes of selling my cargo, as well to take in wood and water. Never before in these parts, it is for me of interest to observe the place and people. You will take a lemonade that Franci brings? Hola, Franci! This is Señor Pike, Franci, at all times to be admitted to the schooner."

"Pleased to meet you!" said Mr. Bill Hen.

"Servicio de Usted!" said Franci, who did not understand English except when he thought the speaker was likely to interest him; and they sat down to the lemonade.

CHAPTER VII.

THE CAPTIVE.

" FRANCI!" the Skipper called up the companion-way, when his visitor had taken his departure.

" Señor!" said Franci, putting his beautiful head over the rail.

" Bring me here the child, hear thou!"

" Si, Señor," said Franci. He went forward, and pulling aside a pile of canvas that lay carelessly heaped together in a corner of the deck, disclosed the boy John, curled up in a ball, with one monkey in his arms, and the other sitting on his shoulder.

" Here, you, Sir Schoolmaster, the Patron ask for you. I give you my hand to hellup you up! I like to put a knife in you!" he added in Spanish, with an adorable smile.

" You'd get one into yourself before you had time!" said Rento, getting up from the spot where his length had been coiled, and speaking with a slow drawl that lent emphasis to the words. " You ever lay a hand on that boy, and it's the last you lay on anybody,—understand that?"

" Oh, yays!" said Franci, gently, as he pulled John out of the tangle of canvas and ropes. " But I am 'most killed all my life with looking at your ugly face, you old she monkey! A little more killing make not much difference to me."

Rento advanced 🐒ard him with uplifted hand, and the agile Spaniard slipped round the mast and disappeared.

"What was he saying?" asked John, vaguely feeling that something was wrong.

"Nothin', nothin' at all," Rento said, quietly. "He was givin' me some talk, that was all. It's all he has to give, seemin'ly; kind o' fool person he is, Franci; don't ye take no heed what he says. There, go 'long, youngster! the Skipper's lookin' for ye."

At this moment the Skipper's head appeared over the rail, and John became quite sure that he was awake. Dreams were so curious, sometimes, one never knew what would happen in them; and this whole matter of piracy had been so strange and unlooked for that all the while he had been hidden under the sail (where he had retreated by the Skipper's orders as soon as Mr. Bill Hen Pike appeared in the offing), he had been trying to persuade himself that he was asleep, and that the monkeys were dream-monkeys, very lively ones, and that by-and-by he would wake up once more and find himself in bed at Mr. Scraper's.

But now there could be no more doubt! He could not dream Franci, nor the queer things he said; he could not dream Rento, with his kind, ugly face and drawling speech; least of all could he dream the Skipper, who was now looking at him with an amused smile.

Certainly, he did not look in the least like a pirate! In the first place, Malay pirates did not wear anything, except a kind of short petticoat, and something that flew in the air behind them as they ran. For in the geography-book pictures a Malay was always running amuck, with a creese in his hand, and an expression of frantic rage on his countenance. How *could* this be a Malay? Perhaps he might have been in fun! But John was not much used to fun, and it seemed hardly likely that so grave a person as the Skipper would play at pirate. On the whole, the little boy was sadly puzzled; and the Skipper's **first** words did not tend to allay his anxiety.

"Ha! my prisoner!" he said. "That you come here, sir, and sit down by me on the rail. The evening falls, and we will sit here and observe the fairness of the night. Remark that I put no chains on you, Colorado, as in the Malay seas we put them! You can swim, yes?"

John nodded. "I swam across the river last week," said he. "I was going to —" He meant to say, "to rescue some people from pirates, but now this did not seem polite; so he stopped short, but the Skipper took no notice.

"You swim? That is good!" he said. "But Sir Scraper, he cannot swim, I think, my son, so for you there is no rescue, since Rento has pulled in the plank. Are you content, then, to be the captive of the ' Nautilus?'"

John looked up, still sorely puzzled; perhaps he was rather dull, this little boy John, about some things, though he was good at his books. At any rate, there could be no possible doubt of the kindness in the Skipper's face; perhaps he was in fun, after all; and, anyhow, where had he ever been so happy as here since the good mother died? So he answered with right good-will, —

"I like to stay here more than anywhere else in the world. If — if I didn't think Mr. Scraper would be angry and frightened about me, and not know where I was, I should like to stay on board all my life."

"That is right!" said the Skipper, heartily. "That is the prisoner that I like to have. I am not a cruel pirate, as some; I like to make happy my captives. Franci, lemonade, on the after-deck here!" He spoke Spanish, and Franci replied in the same language, with a faint voice expressive of acute suffering.

"I am very sick, Patron. I go to my bed in a desolated condition."

"Come here, and let me look at you!" said the Skipper, imperatively.

"Am I a dog, to fetch drink for this beggar brat?" was Franci's next remark, in a more vigorous tone. "Was it for this that I left San Mateo? Rento is a pig, let him do the pig things. I go to my bed."

He made a motion to go, but the Skipper reached out a long arm, and the next moment the bold youth was dangling over the side of the vessel, clutching at the air, and crying aloud to all the saints in the calendar.

"Shall I let go?" asked the Skipper, in his quiet tone.

"Ah! no, distinguished Patron!" cried Franci. "Let me not go! This water is abominable. Release me, and I will get the lemonade. It is my wish that you may both be drowned in it, but I will get it, — oh, yes, assuredly!"

He was set down, and vanished into the cabin; the Skipper, as if this were the most ordinary occurrence in the world, led the way to the after-rail, and se🟫 him-self, motioning to John to take a place beside him.

"What is the matter with him?" asked the boy, looking after Franci.

"I think him slightly a fool," was the reply, as the Skipper puffed leisurely at his cigar. "His parents, worthy peop🟫ired him to be a sailor, but that he can never be. 🟫 🟫est sailor is one born for that, and for no other thing; also, a sailor can be made, though not of so fine quality; but of Franci, no. I return him after this voyage, with compliments, and he sails no more in the 'Nautilus.' And you, Colorado? How is it with you? You love not at all a vessel, I think?"

There certainly could be no doubt this time that the Skipper was making fun; his face was alive with it, and John could have laughed outright for pleasure.

"I 🟫on't believe you are a Malay, one bit!" said the chil🟫 I'm not sure that you are a pirate at all, but I know y🟫 aren't a Malay."

"Why that, my son?" asked the Skipper, waving the smoke aside, that he might see the child's face the clearer. "Why do you think that? I am not dark enough for a Malay, is it that?"

"No, not that," John admitted. "But — well, you have no creese, and you are not wild, nor — nor fierce, nor cruel."

"But I have the creese!" the Skipper protested. "The

creese, would you see it? It is in the cabin, behind the door, with other arms of piracy. Still, Colorado, it is of a fact that I was not born in Polynesia, no. As to the fierceness and the cruelty, we shall see, my son, we shall see. If I kept you here on the 'Nautilus' always, took you with me away, suffered you no more to live with your gentle Sir Scraper, that would be cruelty, do you think it? That would be a fierce pirate, and a cruel one, who would do that?"

John raised his head, and looked long and earnestly in his friend's face. "Of course, I know you are only in fun," he said, at last, "because dreams don't really come true; but — but that *was* my dream, you know! I think I've dreamed you all my life. At least — well, I never knew just what you looked like, or how you would come; but I always dreamed that some one would come from the sea, and that I should hear about the shells, and know what they were saying when they talk; and —" he paused; but the Skipper patted his shoulder gently, in sign that he understood.

"And — what else, Juan Colorado?" he asked, in what seemed the kindest voice in the world. But the boy John hung his head, and seemed loth to go on.

"There — there was another part to what I dreamed," he said at last. "I guess I won't tell that, please, 'cause, of course, you were only in fun."

"And what the harm to tell it," said the Skipper, lightly, "even if it come not true? Dreams are pretty things; my faith, I love to dream mine self. Tell thy friend, Colorado! tell the dream, all the wholeness of it."

There was no resisting the deep, sweet voice. The little boy raised his head again, and looked frankly into the kind, dark eyes.

"I used to dream that I was taken away!" he said, in a low voice.

"Away? Good!" the Skipper repeated.

"Away," the boy murmured, and his voice grew soft and dreamy. "Away from the land, and the fields where the grass dries up so soon, and winter comes before you are ready to be cold. Some one would come and take me in a ship, and I should live always on the water, and it would rock me like a cradle, and I should feel as if I had always lived there. And I should see the flying-fish and dolphins, and know how the corals grow, and see things under the sea. And nobody would beat me then, and I should not have to split wood when it makes my back ache. That was the other part of my dream."

The Skipper laid his hand lightly on the child's head and smoothed back the red curls. "Who knows?" he said, with a smile. "Who knows what may come of dreams, Colorado? Here the one-half is come true, already at this time. Why not the other?" He turned away as if to change the subject, and took up a piece of the white branching coral that lay at his elbow. "When I gather this," he said in a lighter tone, "it was a day in the last year; I remember well that day! A storm had been, and still the sea was rough a little, but that was of no matter. Along the island shore we were cruising, and I saw through the water, there very clear, fine trees."

" Trees ? " repeated the wondering child.

" Of coral, naturally! " said the Skipper.   " Coral trees, Juan, shining bright, bright, through the green water.

" 'Hola, you ! lower anchor !'

" It is done.   I put on the diving dress.   I take a rope about my waist, I descend.   There a forest I find; very beautiful thing to see.   Here we see green trees, and in your north, in fall of year, bright colours, but there colours of rainbow all the year round.   In one place bright yellow, branch and twig of gold purely; the next, purple of a king's garment, colour of roses, colour of peach-blossom in the spring.   Past me, as I descend, float fans of the fan-coral, lilac, spreading a vine-work, trellis, as your word is.   On the one side are cliffs of mountains, with caves in their sides, and from these caves I see come out many creatures; the band-fish, a long ribbon of silver with rose shining through; the Isabelle fish, it is violet and green and gold, like a queen. Under my feet, see, Colorado! sand white like the snow of your winter, fine, shining with many bright sparks. And this is a garden; for all on every hand flowers are growing.   You have seen a cactus, that some lady keeps very careful in her window, tending that it die not? Yes!   Here is the white ground covered with these flowers completely, only of more size hugely, crimson, pale, the heart of a rose, the heart of a young maiden.   Sea-anemones are these, Colorado, many, many kinds, all very fine to see.   And here, too, on the ground are my shells, not as here, when of their brightness the half is gone for want of the life and the water, but full of gleams very glorious, telling of greatness in their making. Here above the water, my little child, I find persons many who doubt of a great God who maketh all things for good, and to grow in the end better; but to have been under the sea, that is to know that it cannot be otherwise ; a true sailor learns many things that are not fully known upon the land, where one sees not so largely His mercy."

He was silent for a moment, and then went on, the child sitting rapt, gazing at him with eyes which saw all the wonders of which he told.

"All these things I saw through the clear water, as if through purest glass I looked. I broke the branches, which now you see white and cleaned, but then all splendid with these colours whereof I tell you. Many branches I broke, putting them in pouches about my waist and shoulders. At once, I see a waving in the water, over my head ; I look up to see a shark swim slowly round and round, just having seen me, and making his preparations. I have my knife ready, for often have I met this gentleman before. I slip behind the coral tree, and wait ; but he is a stupid beast, the shark, and knows not what to do when I come not out. So up I quickly climb through the branches, with care not to tangle the rope ; he still looking for me at the spot where first he saw me. I gain the top, and with a few pulls of my good Rento on the rope, I am in the boat, and Sir Shark is snapping his teeth alone, very hungry, but not invited to dinner."

" Do you think he was stronger than you?" asked the

little boy. " You re very strong, are n't you ? I should
think you were as strong as sharks, and 'most as strong as
whales."

The Skipper laughed. " Sir Shark is ten times so strong
as any man, let him be of the best, my friend ; but he has
not the strength of head, you understand ; that makes the
difference. And you, could you do that, too ? Could you
keep yourself from fear, when the sea-creatures come about
you, if you should ever be a sailor ? What think you ? "

The child pondered.

" I think I could ! " he said at last.

" I never saw any such things, of course, but I 'm
not afraid of anything that I know about, here on shore.
There was a snake," he went on, lowering his voice, " last
summer there was a snake that lived in a hole by the
school-house, and he was a poison snake, an adder. One
day he crept out of his hole and came into the school-
house, and scared them all 'most to death. The teacher
fainted away, and all the children got up into a corner
on the table, and the snake had the whole floor to
himself. But it looked funny to see them all that way
over a little beast that was n't more than two foot
long; so I thought about it, and then I went to the
wood-box (we were burning brushwood then) and got a
stick with a little fork at the end, and I came up quick
behind the snake, and clapped that down over his neck, so
he could n't turn his head round, and then I took another
stick and killed him. That 's only a little thing, but I
was n't afraid at all, and I thought perhaps it would show

whether I would be good for anything when there were real things to be afraid of."

The Skipper nodded in his pleasant, understanding way. "I think so, too, Colorado," he said. "I think so, too! That was like my boy Rento, but not like Franci. Franci dies every time he see a snake, and come to life only to find out if somebody else is killed. See, my son, how beautiful the moon on the water! Let us look for a few moments, to take the beauty into us, and then I must send my little friend to his bed, that nothing harmful comes to him."

So they sat hand in hand for awhile, gazing their fill, saying nothing; there was the same look in the two faces, so widely different. The little boy, with his clear brow, his blue eyes limpid as a mountain pool, shining with the heavens reflected in them ; the dark Spaniard (if he were a Spaniard!) with lines of sadness, shadows of thought and of bitter experience, making his bronze face still darker; what was there alike in these two, who had come together from the ends of the earth? The thought was one, in both hearts, and the look of it shone in the eyes of both as they sat in the moonlight white and clear. What was the thought? Look into the face of your child as it kneels to pray at close of day! Look into the face of any good and true man when he is lifted above the things of to-day, and sees the beauty and the mystery, and hears the eternal voices sounding!

> "'Morning, evening, noon and night,
> Praise God!' sang Theocrite."

CHAPTER VIII.

IN THE NIGHT.

THE evening had been peaceful, all beauty and silence; but not so the night for the boy John. Something was the matter; he could not sleep. The bunk in the little cabin was comfortable enough for anyone, but to him it was a couch for an emperor. He speculated on the probability of George the Third's having had anything like so luxurious a bed, and rejected the thought as absurd. There were no lumps in the mattress, neither any holes through which sharp fingers of straw came out and scratched him. The red curtains at the sides could be drawn at will, and, drawing them, he found himself in a little world of his own, warm and still and red. The shells were outside in the other world; he could look out at any moment and see them, and touch them, take them up; his friend had said so. Now, however, it seemed best just to be alive, and to stay still and wonder what would become of him. He heard the Skipper come down and go to bed, and soon the sound of deep, regular breathing told that he slept, the man of wonder; but John could not sleep. And now other thoughts came thronging into his mind, thoughts that were not soft and crimson and luxurious. To go away, as the Skipper had said, — to go to heaven! But one did not go to heaven till the time came. Was it right? Was the Skipper a good man?

The child debated the question with anguish, lying with wide open eyes in his crimson-shaded nest. Mr. Scraper was — not — very nice, perhaps; but he had taken him, John, when his mother died, and fed and clothed him. He had often had enough to eat — almost enough — and — and Mr. Scraper was old, and perhaps pretty soon his legs would go to sleep, like old Captain Baker's, and he would not be able to walk at all, and then how would it be if he were left alone? Perhaps people would not come to help him, as they had helped the captain, because everybody in the village loved the captain, and no one exactly loved Mr. Scraper. So if the only person who belonged to him at all should go off and leave him, how could it be expected that the folks who had their own grandfathers and things to take care of would stop and go to take care of this old man? And if he should die there, all alone, with no one to read to him or bring him things, or feed him with a spoon, why, — how would it seem to himself, the boy John's self, when he should hear of it?

" I am a murderer ! " he said aloud; and straightway, at the sound of his own voice, cowered under the bedclothes, and felt the hangman's hand at his neck.

What did it mean, when a person could not sleep?

There was a man in an old book there at the house, and he was wicked, and he never could sleep, never at all. The things he had done came and sat on him, and they were hot, like coals, and the heat went through to his heart and

burned it. Would it be so with him, if he should go away
in the "Nautilus," and forget — or try to forget — the old
man who had nobody to love him? Not that Mr. Scraper
wanted to be loved yet, at all; but — but he might, some
time, when his legs had gone to sleep, and then —

Sometimes, when a person could not sleep, it meant that
he was going to die. Suppose one were to die now, and go
to heaven, and they said to one, " How was Mr. Scraper
when you came away?" and one had to say, " I ran away
and left him this evening, and I don't know how he is, or
whether he is alive or dead — for sometimes old people die
just like that, dropping down in their chairs — what would
they say to one? Perhaps the old man had dropped down
now, this very night, from anger at his being away when
he should have done the chores. He saw Mr. Scraper
sitting in his arm-chair, cold and dead, with the rats running over the floor at his feet, because he, John, had
not set the trap. A scream rose to his lips, but he choked
it back; and sitting up in desperation, drew aside the red
curtains and looked out.

The cabin lay dim and quiet before him. A lantern
hung in the middle, turned low, and by its light he could
see the shelves, with their shining rows of shells, and the
glass counter with the sea-jewelry. Directly opposite him,
only the narrow space of the cabin between, lay the
Skipper in his bunk, sleeping peacefully. The wild fear
died away in the child's heart as he saw the calmness and
repose of the stalwart figure. One arm was thrown out;
the strong, shapely hand lay with the palm open toward

him, and there was infinite cheer and hospitality in the
attitude. In the dim light the Skipper's features looked
less firm and more kind; yet they were always kind. It
was not possible that this was a bad man, a stealer of children, a pilferer of old men's cupboards.

If one could think that he had been playing all the
time, making believe, just as a person did one's self; but
John had never known any grown people who could make
believe; they had either forgotten, or else they were
ashamed of the knowledge. Once, it was true, he had
persuaded Mr. Bill Hen Pike to be Plymouth Rock, when
he wanted to land in the "Mayflower;" but just as the
landing was about to be effected, Mrs. Pike had called
wrathfully from the house, and the rock sprang up and
shambled off without even a word of apology or excuse.
So grown people did not understand these things, probably;
and yet, — yet if it had been play, what glorious times
one could have, with a real creese, and a real schooner,
and everything delightful in the world!

How could he be bad and look like that? The child
bent forward and strained his eyes on the sleeping face.
So quiet, so strong, so gentle! He tried putting other
faces beside it, for he saw faces well, this boy, and remembered what he had seen. He tried Mr. Scraper's face, with
the ugly blink to the red eyes, and the two wrinkles
between the eyes, and the little nest of spiteful ones that
came about his mouth when he was going to be angry;
even when he slept—the old gentleman—his hands were
clenched tight—how different from that open palm, with

its silent welcome! — and his lips pursed up tight. No! no! that was not a pleasant picture! Well, there was Lena! she was pleasant to look at, surely! Her hair was like silver, and her eyes blue and soft, though they could be sharp, too. But, somehow, when her face was brought here beside the Skipper's, it looked foolish and empty, and her pretty smile had nothing to say except to bid one look and see how pretty she was, and how becoming blue was to her; and — and, altogether, she would not do at all.

Mr. Bill Hen, then, who was always kind to him, and quite often, when Mrs. Pike was not near, would give him a checkerberry lozenge. Mr. Bill Hen's face was good-natured, to be sure, but oh, how coarse and red and stupid it was beside the fine dark sleeping mask! Why did people look so different, and more when they were asleep than any other time? Did one's soul come out and kind of play about, and light up the person's face; and if so, was it not evident that the Skipper *was* a good man? and that perhaps things were really different in his country, and they had other kinds of Ten Commandments, and — no, but right was right, and it did n't make any difference about countries in that sort of thing. You knew that yourself, because you felt it in your stomach when you did bad things; perhaps when one grew older, one's stomach did not feel so quickly. And, anyhow, if that was true about the soul, how do you suppose a person's own soul would make his face look if he was running away from the things he ought to do, and going to play with monkeys and see the wonders of the world? The boy wondered what he was looking like at the present moment, and summoned up the image of a frightful picture of a devil in another of those old books into which he was forever peeping at odd times. Did they miss him now, the old books in the garret, because he had not come up to wish them good-night and take a look at some of the best pictures before he went to bed? Was he likely to turn into a devil when he died, do you suppose?

How still it was, and how queer his eyes felt! But he could not lie down, for then he would be alone again, and the things would come and sit on him; it was good to sit up and look at the Skipper, and wonder — and wonder —

A gleam, faint and red, shot from a shell in the farther corner, — a splendid creature, scarlet and pale green, with horns that gave it a singularly knowing look. He almost thought it nodded to him; and hark! was that a tiny voice speaking, calling him by name?

" Come away, little boy!" said the voice. " Come away to the south, where the water is blue always, and storms come rarely, rarely! There, under the water, my brothers and sisters wait to see you, and with them their friends, the lovely ones, of whom you have dreamed all your life. There, on beds of sea-moss, they lie, and the rainbow is dull beside them. Flowers are there, and stars, and bells that wave softly without sound. For one fair thing that the man, our master, told you of, we have a thousand to show you. What does he know, a man, whose eyes are already half-shut? But you are a child, and for you all things shall be opened under the ocean, and you

shall see the treasures of it, and the wonders; and you
shall grow wise, wise, so that men shall look up to you,
and shall say, ' Where did he gain his knowledge?' And
your friend shall be with you, oh yes, for he knows the
way, if he cannot see all the things that will meet your
eyes! And you and he together shall sail — shall sail,
through waters green as chrysoprase; and all the sea-
creatures shall learn to know you and love you. You
shall learn where the sea-otter makes his nest, in the
leaves of the giant sea-weed, where they stretch along
the water, full sixty feet long, as the Skipper told you.
The ' Nautilus ' will be there, too: not a clumsy wooden
mountain, like this in which we lie prisoned, but the creature itself, the fairy thing of pearl and silver! Look! here
lies his shell, and you find it lovely; but like us, it is dim
and dead for want of the life within it.

" Come away, and let us be sailing, sailing over seas of
gold! And when you are weary of the top of the waves,
down you shall sink with us through the clear green water,
and the night will fall like a soft dream, and the moon-
fish, with its disk of silver, shall gleam beside you to light
the dimness that yet is never dark; and you shall go
down, down, down — "

And about this time it must have been that the little
boy went down, for when the morning broke, the Skipper
found him, fast asleep, and smiling as he slept.

CHAPTER IX.

FAMILY MATTERS.

"WELL," said Mr. Bill Hen, "I only want to put it to you, you understand. Intelligent man like you, no need for me to do more than put it to you. There's the child, and there's the old man, and they 'pear to have got separated. I don't want to be understood as implying anything, not anything in the living world; but there's where it is, you see. And me being a justice of the peace, and sworn, you observe, to — well, I'm sure you will see for yourself the position I'm placed in. Point is, you seemed consid'able interested in the child, as one may say. Nothing strange in that, — nice little boy! would interest an Injin chief, if he had any human feelin' in him. But *bein'* a justice of the peace, you see, — well, Mr. Scraper has sent me to make inquiries, and no offence in the world, I trust — no in*sult*, you understand, if I jest — well, all about it — do you know where in thunder the child is ?"

Mr. Bill Hen, standing on the bank, delivered himself of these remarks with infinite confusion, perspiring freely, and wiping his face with a duster, which he had brought by mistake instead of a handkerchief. He looked piteously at the Skipper, who stood leaning over the side, cheerfully inscrutable, clad in spotless white, and smoking a long cigar.

"The child?" the Skipper repeated, thoughtfully. "You allude to the boy called John, Señor Pike; yes, I had that suppose. Now, sir, the day before this, you tell me that this child is not well placed by that old gentleman Scraper; that the old man is cruel, is base, is a skin-the-flint, shortly. You tell me this, and I make reply to you that there are powers more high than this old person, who have of that child charge. How, if those powers had delivered to me the child? how then, I ask you, Señor Pike?"

Mr. Bill Hen wiped his brow again and gasped feebly. "'Tis as I thought!" he said. "You've got the child aboard."

The Skipper nodded, and blew rings from his cigar. "I have the child," he repeated, "aboard. What will you in this case do, Señor? I propose to take him with me away, to make of him a sailor, to care for him as my son. You think well of this; you have been kind to the child always, as he tell me? You are glad to have him remove from the slavery of this old fish, yes?" He smiled, and bent his dark eyes on his unhappy visitor.

Mr. Bill Hen writhed upon the hook. "There — there's truth in what you say," he admitted, at length, after seeking counsel in vain from his red bandanna. "There's truth in what you say, I aint denyin' that. But what I look at, you see, is my duty. You may have your idees of duty, and I may have mine; and I'm a justice of the peace, and I don't see anything for it but to ask you to give up that child to his lawful guardeen, as has sent me for him."

A pause ensued, during which Franci sauntered to the side with easy grace. "Shall I put a knife into him, Patron?" he asked, indicating Mr. Bill Hen with a careless nod. "How well he would stick, ch? The fatness of his person! It is but to say the word, Patron."

Mr. Bill Hen recoiled with a look of horror, and prepared for instant flight; but the Skipper's gesture reassured him. "Franci, look if there is a whale on the larboard bow!" said the latter.

"Perfectly, Patron!" replied Franci, withdrawing with his most courtly bow. "When I say that no one will be killed at all in this cursed place, and I shall break my heart! but as you will."

Again there was a pause, while Mr. Bill Hen wondered if this were a floating lunatic asylum or a nest of pirates, that had come so easily up their quiet river and turned the world topsy-turvy. At length — "Your force, Señor Pike," the Skipper said, "I perceive it not, for to take away this child. Have you the milizia — what you call soldiers, police — have you them summoned and concealed behind the rocks, as in the theatres of Havana? I see no one but your one self. Surely you have no thought to take the child of your own force from me?"

Mr. Bill Hen gasped again. "Look here!" he broke out at last. "What kind of man are you, anyway? you aint no kind that we're used to in these parts, so now I tell you. When a man hears what is law in this part of the world, he gives in, as is right and proper, to that law and that — and — and in short to them sentiments. Are you going to stand out against the law, and keep that child? and who give you a right to do for that child? I suppose I can ask that question, if you are a grandee, or whatever you are. Who give you a right, I ask?"

"Who shall say?" replied the Skipper. "Perhaps — " He said no more, but raised his hand with a gesture that was solemn enough; and Mr. Bill Hen Pike decided that he was beyond doubt a madman. But now the Skipper dropped his tone and attitude of smiling ease, and, throwing away his cigar, stood upright. "Enough, Señor!" he said. "You are a good man, but you have not the courage. Now, you shall see Colorado." He turned toward the cabin and called: "Colorado, my son, come to me!" Then, after a pause, "He sleeps yet. Rento, bring to me the child!" Rento, who had been hovering near, lending a careful ear to all that was said, now vanished, and re-appeared, bearing the boy John in his arms. The child was but newly awake, and was still rubbing his eyes and looking about him in bewilderment.

"Colorado, the Señor Pike, already well known to you!" said the Skipper, with a graceful wave of the hand. "Your guardian, the old gentleman Scraper, desires of our company at breakfast. How then, son of mine? Shall we go, or shall I keep you here, and bid Sir Scraper find his way to the devil, which will be for him little difficult?" He smiled on the boy, and took his hand with a caressing gesture.

Little John heaved a great sigh, and the cares of the world floated from him like a summer cloud. "Oh, I knew it!" he cried, smiling joyously up into his friend's face. "I knew it all the time, or almost all! You never meant anything but fun, did you? and we will go back, won't we? And we shall feel all right inside, and things will not sit — I — I mean nothing will feel bad any more. I — I can't say all I mean," he added, rather lamely, "because I 'had thoughts in the night; but we will go now, you and I, you and I!"

. . . .

As they approached the gate, John stopped a moment, and looked up at his companion. " Would you mind holding my hand?" he asked. "I am all right in my mind, but I think I am rather queer in my legs ; I think I should feel better if I held the hand of — of somebody who was n't little, or — or weak."

Oh, the strong, cordial pressure of the big, brown hand! how it sent warmth and cheer and courage through the little quivering frame! John was all right in his mind, as he said, but his body felt already the stinging blows of the cane, his ears rang already with the burning words of rage and spite.

" But it is the inside that matters!" said John, aloud ; and he shut his eyes and went into the house.

" Good-morning, gentleman," the Skipper began, always at his courteous ease.

" I have to ask your forgiveness, that I carry off yesterday our young friend here. You were not at house, I desired greatly of his company; I have the ways of the sea, waiting not too long for the things I like; briefly, I take him away. That I bear the blame of this is my desire. And now, shall we pleasantly converse, ha?"

He seated himself, drew the boy between his knees, and looked Mr. Scraper squarely in the eyes. Now, Mr. Scraper did not like to be looked at in this manner; he shifted on his chair, and his mouth, which had been opened to pour out a flood of angry speech, closed with a spiteful snap, and then opened, and then closed again.

The Skipper observed these fish-like snappings with grave attention. At length, —

"Who are you, I should like to know?" the old man cried in an angry twitter.

"Why in — why do you come meddling here, and carrying off boys from their lawful guardeens, and talking folderol, and raising Ned generally? I've seen skippers before, but I never heered of no such actions as these, never in my days! Why, no one here so much as knows your name; and here you seem to own the hull village, all of a sudden. You, John," he added, with a savage snarl, "you go about your business, and I'll see to you afterwards. I reckon you won't go out again without leave for one while!"

The child started obediently, but the strong hand held him fast.

"Quiet, Colorado," said the Skipper. "Quiet, my son! Time enough for the work, plenty time! I desire you here now, see you." Then he turned once more to the old man.

"You have, I already say, a beautiful name, Sir Scraper," he said with cheerful interest. "Endymion! a fine name, truly — of poetry, of moonlight and beauty; you have had great joy of that name, I cannot doubt?"

"What's my name to you, I should like to know?" retorted Mr. Scraper, with acrimony. "This aint the first time you 've took up my name, and I 'll thank you to leave it alone! You let go that boy, or I 'll let you know more 'n you knew before."

"Perfectly!" said the Skipper. "Attend but a moment, dear sir. Let us pursue for a moment thoughts of poetry! Such a name as Endymion proves a poetic fancy in the giver of it; at a guess, this was your lady mother, now probably with the saints, and if others so fortunate as to belong to your family, surely this excellent lady would have given to them, also, names of soul, of poetry! If there was a sister, for example, would she be named Susan? No! Jane? Never! Find me then a name! Come! at a venture. Zenobia? Aha! what say you?"

He leaned forward, and his glance was like the flash of a sword. The child looked in wonder from one to the other; for the old man had sunk back in his chair, and his jaw had fallen open in·an ugly way, and altogether he was a sad object to look at.

"What — what d' ye mean?" he gasped, after a moment. But the Skipper went on, speaking lightly and cheerfully, as if talking of the weather.

"What pleasure to bring before the mind a picture of a family so charming! Of you, dear sir, in your gra-

cious childhood, how endearing the image! how tenderly
guarded, how fondly cherished here by your side the little
sister?   Ah! the smiling picture, making glad the heart!
This sister, Zenobia, let us say, grows up, after what
happy childhood with such a brother needs for me not to
say.   They are three, these children, — how must they love
each other!   But one brother goes early away from the
home!   In time comes for Zenobia, as to young maidens
will come, a suitor, a foreigner, shall we say? a man, like
myself, of the sea?   May it not have been possible, dear
sir?"

"A roving nobody!" the old man muttered, striving to
pull himself together.   "A   rascally" — but here he
stopped abruptly, for a stern hand was laid on his arm.

"I am speaking at this present, sir!" said the Skipper.
"Of this man I do not ask you the character.   I tell my
story, if you please, in my own way.

"The mother, by this time, is dead.   The father, unwill-
ing to part with his daughter, — alas! the parental heart,
how must it be torn?   As yours, the tender one, last night,
on missing this beloved child, Sir Scraper.   The father,
I say, opposes the marriage; at length only, and after
many tears, much sorrow, some anger, consents; the
daughter, sister, Zenobia, goes with her husband away,
promising quickly to return, to take her old father to her
home in the southern islands.   Ah, the interesting tale,
is it not?   Observe, Colorado, my son, how I am able to
move this, your dear guardian.   The pleasant thing, to
move the mind of age, so often indifferent.

Zenobia goes away, and the son, the good son, the one faithful and devoted, who will not marry, so great his love for his parent, is left with that parent alone. How happy can we fancy that parent, is it not? How gay for him the days, how sweet for him the nights, lighted with love, and smoothed his pillow by loving hands, — ah, the pleasant picture! But how, my friend, you feel yourself not well? Colorado, a glass of water for your guardian."

The old man motioned the child back, his little eyes gleaming with rage and fear.

" You — you come a-nigh me, you brat, and I 'll wring your neck!" he gasped. " Well, Mister, have you finished your — your story, as you call it? Why do I want to listen to your pack of lies, I should like to know? I wonder I 've had patience to let you go on so long."

" Why do you want to listen?" the Skipper repeated. " My faith, do I know? But the appearance of interest in your face so venerable, it touch me to the heart. Shall I go and tell the rest of my story to him there, that other, the justice of the peace? But no, it would break your heart to hear not the end. That we proceed then, though not so cheerful the ending of my story. Zenobia, in her southern home, happy, with her child at her knee, feels still in her heart the desire to see once more her father, to bring him to her, here in the warm south to end his days of age. She writes, but no answer comes; again she writes, and again, grief in her soul, to think that anger is between her and one so dear. At last, after a long time, a letter from her brother, the stay-at-home, the faithful

one ; their father is dead; is dead,— without speaking of
her; the property is to him left, the faithful son.   It is
finished, it is concluded, the earth is shut down over the
old man, and no more is to say.

"With what tender, what loving words this cruel news
tells itself, needs not to repeat to a person so of feeling as
yourself, Sir Scraper.   Zenobia, sad woman, believes what
she is told; bows her head, gathers to her closer her husband and her son, and waits the good time when God
shall make to her good old father the clear knowledge
that she has always loved him.   Ah, yes, my faith!

"Now, in a year, two years, I know not, what arrives?
A letter, old and worn; a letter soiled, discoloured, of
carrying long in a sailor's pocket, but still easily to be
read.   This letter — shall we guess, Sir Scraper?   Well,
then, from her father!   The old man in secret, in fear,
lying on his bed of death, makes come by stealth a neigh-
bour, kindly disposed to him; makes write by his hand
this letter; makes draw up besides, it may be, other
papers, what do we know?

"Ah! but remain quiet, dear sir.   Grieved that I do
not interest you, I must still pray of your presence, that
you do not yet withdraw it.   Ancient fish-skin, do I tie
thee in thy chair?

"So! that is well, and you will remain quiet, Señor,
with a thousand pardons!

"This letter, then, it is one to wring the heart.   He has
longed for his daughter, this poor old man; in two grasp-
ing hands held as in a vise, he turns to her who was

always kind, he prays her to return, to let him come to her, what she will. Failing this, and knowing that on earth the time is short for him to remain, he bids her not grieve, but send to her home a messenger of trust, and let him look for a certain paper, in a certain place. Finally, he prays for her the blessing of God, this good old man, and bids her farewell, if he may never see her more. Truly, a letter over which a pirate, even a Malay pirate, Colorado of my heart, might shed tears."

The Skipper's voice was still quiet, but its deep tones were stern with suppressed feeling; with menace, was it? The child, bewildered, looked from one to the other of his two companions. The Spaniard's eyes burned red in their depths, his glance seemed to pierce marrow and sinew; he sat leaning lightly forward in his chair, alert, possessing himself, ready for any sudden movement on the part of his adversary; for the old man must be his adversary; something deadly must lie between these two. Mr. Scraper lay back in his chair like one half dead, yet the rage and spite and hatred, the baffled wonder, the incredulity struggling with what was being forced upon him, made lively play in his sunken face. His lean hands clutched the arms of the chair as if they would rend the wood; his frame shook with a palsy. Little John wondered what could ail his guardian; yet his own heart was stirred to its depths by what he had heard.

"The son was bad!" he cried. "He was a bad man! Things must have sat upon his breast *all* night, and I am sure he could not sleep at all. Are you sorry for a person who is as bad as that? do you think any one tried to help him to be better?"

But the Skipper raised his finger, and pointed to the evil face of the old man.

" Does that man look as if he slept, my son?" he asked.

" Listen always, and you shall hear the last of the story."

" It 's a lie!" Mr. Scraper screamed at last, recovering the power of speech.

" It 's a lie that you 've cooked up from what you have heard from the neighbours. May their tongues rot out! And if it were true as the sun, what is it to you? She 's dead, I tell you! She 's been dead these twenty years! I had the papers telling of her death; I 've got 'em now, you fool."

" Quiet then, my uncle!" said the Skipper, bending forward, and laying his hand on the old man's knee.

"She is dead, she died in these arms. I am her son, do you see?"

But if Mr. Scraper saw, it was only for a moment, for he gave a scream, and fell together sideways in his chair, struck with a fit.

CHAPTER X.

IN THE VALLEY OF DECISION.

" AND now, Colorado, son of my heart," the Skipper said, " you understand why I was a thief that yesterday, and why I could not permit you at that instant to tell of my thieving ? "

They had put the old man to bed, and Mr. Bill Hen had gone for the doctor. In fact, when John ran out of the door, he had found Mr. Bill Hen leaning up against it, as speechless, with amazement and confusion, as Mr. Scraper himself! The good man, wholly unable to restrain his curiosity, had followed the Skipper and the boy, unbeknown to them, and posting himself in a convenient angle of the porch, had heard every word of the conversation. The Skipper, perceiving the facts, managed to rouse him with a few sharp words, and sent him off in hot haste to the village; and had then proceeded to make the old gentleman comfortable, and to set things shipshape, so far as might be.

" Do you think he will die ? " asked John, peeping over the bed at the sunken features of the old man.

" I do not! " was the reply.

" I think this my revered uncle has yet many years to live — and repent, if so he be minded. He is a very bad old man, Colorado, this my revered uncle! Ah, thou ancient fish, thou art finally landed!"

"Are you sorry for a person when he is so bad as that?" asked the boy, as he had asked once before.

"Do you think a person could make him better, if he tried very hard indeed?"

"I have no knowledge!" said the Skipper, rather shortly. "I am a human person altogether, my son! and I concern myself not greatly with the improvement of this my revered uncle. Behold it, the will, made by my grandfather, the father of my poor mother, whose soul, with his, rest in eternal glory! By this, my mother, and I after her, inherit this house, this garden, these possessions such as they are. If I desire, son of mine, I may come here to-day to live, sell the 'Nautilus,' or cut her cable and let her drift down the river, with Rento and Franci, and all the shells; and I may live here in my house, to — what do you say? cultivate my lands, cat grass and give it to the cattle? What think you, Colorado? Is that a life? Shall I lead it, as is my right? Have I not had enough, think you, of roving over the sea, with no place where I may rest, save the heaving ocean, that rests never beneath the foot? Shall we turn out this old wicked man, who did to death his old father, who made my mother go sad of heart to her grave, who has done of all his life no kind act to any person — shall we turn him out, and live in peace here, you and I?"

The child came near to him, and laid his hand on his friend's knee, and looked up in his face with troubled eyes.

"I am not very bright," he said, "and you think so

many things so quickly that I do not know what you mean a good deal of the time. But — but Cousin Scraper took me when my people died, and he has taken care of me ever since, and — and he has no one else to take care of him now."

"Yes, the fine care he has taken of you!" said the Skipper. "You are of skin and bone, my child, and there are marks on your skin of blows, I saw them yesterday: cruel blows, given from a bad heart. You have worked for him, this ancient fish-skin, how long? Of wages, how much has he paid you? Tell me these things, and I will tell you how much it is your duty to stay by him."

But John shook his head, and the shadows deepened in his blue eyes.

"You cannot tell a person those things," he said; "a person has to tell himself those things. But thank you all the same," he added, fervently; "and I love you always more and more, every day and every minute, and I always shall."

"Now the question is," said the Skipper, shrugging his shoulders in mock despair, "must I turn pirate in truth, to gain possession of a child whom I could hold in my pocket, and who would give all his coloured hair from his head to go with me? Go away, son of mine, that I reflect on these things, for you try my soul!"

John withdrew, very sad, and wondering how it was that right and wrong could ever get mixed. He thought of looking in some of the old books to see, but, somehow, books did not appeal to him just now. He went up to his own little

room, and took down the china poodle, and had a long talk
with him; that was very consoling, and he felt better after
it; it was wonderful how it cleared the mind to talk a
thing over with an old friend.   The poodle said little, but
his eyes were full of sympathy, and that was the main
thing.   By-and-by, as the child sat by his little window,
polishing the pearl-shell on his sleeve, and thinking over
the strange events of the last few days, there came to him
from below the sound of voices.   The doctor was there,
evidently; perhaps Mr. Bill Hen, too; and little as he felt
inclined to merriment, John fell into a helpless laughter, as
he recalled the look of that worthy man when he was discovered flattened against the door.   How much older one
grew sometimes in a short time!   Mr. Bill Hen used to look
so old, so wise, and now he seemed no more than another
boy, and perhaps rather a foolish boy.   But seeing the
Skipper made a great difference in a person's life.

Presently the door at the foot of the stairs opened, and
John heard his name called; he hastened down, and found
Mr. Scraper sitting up in bed, looking pale and savage, but
in full possession of his faculties.   The doctor was there,
a burly, kind-eyed man, and Mr. Bill Hen was there, and
the Skipper; and when little John entered, they all looked
at him, and no one said anything for a moment.

At length the doctor broke the silence.

" I understand, sir," he said, addressing the Skipper,
" that you have a paper, a will or the like, substantiating
your claims ? "

" I have ! " the Skipper replied.   " The letter received by my mother, shortly before her death, was dictated by my grandfather, and told that, hearing for many years nothing from his son, this child's grandfather, he had made a will in her favour. This, being timorous, he had not dared to show to anyone, neither to send her a copy, but he bade her send a messenger to make search in a certain cupboard of this house, on a certain shelf, where would be found this paper. My mother dying, commended to me this search. I at that time was a youth on adventures bent, with already plans for eastern voyages. Keeping always the letter in my pouch, and in my heart the desire of my mother, I came, nevertheless, not to this part of the world; years come and go, Señor, swiftly with men of the sea, and these shores seemed to me less of attraction than Borneo and other places where were easily to be found my wares. Briefly, I came not; till this year, a commission from a collector of some extent brought the 'Nautilus' to New York. And then, say I, how then if I go on, see this my inheritance, discover if it may profit me somewhat? I come, I discover my revered uncle, unknown to him. Is the discovery such that I desire to fall on his respected bosom, crying, 'My uncle, soul of my family, behold your son!' I ask you, Señors both! But I find this, my revered uncle, to be a collector of shells: thus he is in one way already dear to my heart. Again, I find here at the moment of my arrival a child, who is in effect of my own blood, who is to me a son from the moment of our first speech. Is it so, Colorado? Speak, my child!"

John could not speak, but he nodded like a little

mandarin, and the red curls fell into his eyes and hid the tears, so that no one but the Skipper saw them.

"How then?" the Skipper resumed, after a moment's pause. "My soul not calling me to reveal myself to this so-dear relative, what do I? I come to this house, without special plan, to spy out the land, do we say? I find my uncle forth of the house; I find my child travailing in the garden. Good! The time appears to me accepted. I enter, I search, I find the cupboard, I find the paper. Briefly, Señors both, behold me possessor of this house, this garden, this domain royal."

He handed a paper to the doctor, who read it carefully, and nodded. Mr. Scraper made an attempt to clutch it in passing, but grasped the air only.

"What then, in finality, do I say?" the Skipper went on. "Do I desire to stay in this place? Wishing not to grieve the Señor Pike, whom greatly I esteem, I consider it unfit for the human being. Of property, I have little desire; I have for my wants enough, I have my 'Nautilus,' I have my boys, to what end should I retain these cold spots of earth, never before seen by me? To what purpose, I ask it of you, Señors? Therefore, in finality, I say to my revered uncle this: Give to me the child, give to me the boy, that I take away and make a sailor, for which he was born; and I of my part surrender house and garden, even any money bags which may be, what know I, perhaps at this moment in the bed of my revered uncle concealed?"

The old man gave a convulsive shudder at this, and shrieked faintly; all started, but the Skipper laughed.

",You see, Señor Pike, and Señor Doctor, greatly respected! Who shall know how great sums this ancient fish has hidden under him? Let him keep them, these sums. I take the child, and I go my way. Is it finished, uncle of my heart? Is it finished, venerable iniquity? Can you part with the child, beloved, even as your old father was beloved, and like him caressed and tenderly entreated? Answer, thou!"

But before Mr. Scraper could speak, little John stepped forward, very pale, but clear in his mind.

"If you please," he said, "I should like to speak. If you please, he (indicating the Skipper,) is so kind, and—and—he knows what I—he knows things I have thought about, but he does not know all. Cousin Scraper, you may be sick now, perhaps a long time, and perhaps you have gone upon your bed to die, like that king in the Bible who had figs put on; only he got well.

"And I want to stay and take care of you, and—and I will do as well as I know how, and I think I can work more than I used to, because I know more, these last days, than I did, and—and—I think that is all. But if you don't mind—if you would try to like me a little, I think we should get on better; and if dried figs would do, we might try those, you know."

Here he turned to the doctor, with a face of such clear brightness that the good man choked, and coughed, and finally went and looked out of the window, wondering whether he was laughing or crying.

Then John came forward, and held out both hands to the old man with an appealing gesture.

" Will you try to like me a little ? " he said; and for the first time his voice quivered.

" For now my only friend is going away, and I am sending him, and I shall never see him again."

Mr. Endymion Scraper was a man of few ideas; and only one was in his mind at this moment. Gathering himself up in the bed, he pushed the boy away from him with all his feeble strength.

" Go 'way! " he said. " Go 'way, I tell ye. If that man there will take ye, he's welcome to ye, I guess. If he's fool enough to take ye in exchange for property, saying the property was his, which I aint fool enough to do without a lawyer — he's welcome to ye. I say, he's welcome. I don't want no brats round here. I took ye out of charity, and I've had enough of ye. Go 'long, I say, with that wuthless feller, if he is my sister's son. I want to be rid of the hull lot and passel of ye! "

His voice rose to a scream, and the veins on his narrow forehead stood out like cords. The doctor motioned to the Spaniard; and the latter, without another word, took the child up in his arms as he had done once before, swung him over his shoulder, and left the room.

CHAPTER XI

"R ENTO!"
  "Ay, ay, sir!"
"Franci!"
"Señor!"
"Jack and Jim!"

The monkeys for answer leaped on their master's shoulder, and chattered, and peered round into his face.

"The company of this schooner, attention! Behold Colorado, who comes to be my son! He sails with us, he receives kindness from you all, he is in his home. Instruction you will give him in ways of the sea, and he becomes in all things your brother. Am I understood?"

The different members of the crew received this intelligence each in his own way. Rento advanced, and shaking John cordially by the hand, assured him with honest warmth that he was proper glad to see him, and that he hoped they should be good friends.

Franci smiled like an angel, and the moment the Skipper's back was turned, made frightful grimaces at the boy, and threatened his life. But John was too happy to be afraid of Franci. Going boldly up to him, he asked,—

"Why don't you like me, and why do you want to kill

me? I never did you any harm, and I should like to be friends, please."

The Spaniard looked at him sidelong out of his soft, sleepy eyes.

"Have you understanding?" he asked presently. "Have you intelligence to accept the idea of a person of poetry, of soul?"

"I think so!" said John, with some confidence. "I could try, anyhow."

"Look, then!" exclaimed Franci, throwing his arms abroad with a dramatic gesture.

"I am not of nature murderous. A dove, a lamb at sport in the meadow, such is the heart of Franci. But— behold me desolated on this infernal schooner. Torn by my parents from my home, from warm places of my delight, from various maidens, all enamoured of my person, I am sent to be a sailor. A life of horror, believe me who say it to you! Wetness, cold and work; work, cold and wetness! Behold the sea! may it be accursed, and dry up at the earliest moment! I come here, on this so disastrous voyage. Have I poetry, think you, on board this vessel? Is the pig-faced armadillo yonder a companion for me, for Franci? Is my beauty, the gentleness and grace of my soul appreciated here? even the Patron, a person in some ways of understanding, has for me only the treatment of a child, of a servant. Crushed to the ground by these afflictions, how do I revenge myself? How do I make possible the passage of time in this wooden prison? I make for myself the action, I make for myself the theatre.

Born for the grace of life, deprived of it, let me have the horrors! In effect, 1 would not hurt the safety of a flea; in appearance, I desire blood, blood, blood!"

He shrieked the last words aloud, and leaped upon the boy, his eyes glaring like a madman's; but John was on his own ground now; his eyes shone with appreciation. " That's splendid!" he cried. " Blood! Oh, I wish I could do it like that! 1 say, we can play all kind of things, can't we? We'll be pirates — only good pirates, — and we'll scour the seas, and save all the shipwrecked people, won't we? And you shall be the captain (or you might call it admiral, if you liked the sound better, I often do), and I will be the mate, or the prisoners, or the drowning folks, just as you like. I love to play things."

" Come to my heart, angelic child!" cried Franci, flinging out his arms once more. " At length I am understood, I am appreciated, I have found a comrade! That I weep on thy bosom, Colorado!"

And, much to the disgust of Rento, he fell upon John's neck, and shed, or appeared to shed, a few tears, with great parade of silk handkerchief. He then advanced to where the Skipper was smoking his cigar in the stern, and informed him, with a low bow, that he and Colorado were one soul, which the Skipper said he was delighted to hear, adding that he recommended the one soul to set the two bodies to work cleaning the brasses.

Franci liked to clean the brasses, because he could see his face in them, and make eyes at himself as he went along; accordingly he turned three back-somersaults, a sign of high good-humour with him, and returned to his new friend.

" Have you noticed, Colorado," he inquired, " the contour of my leg ? Did you observe it now, quivering in the air ? "

John nodded appreciation, and wondered how old Franci was.

" To possess beauty," said the latter, gravely, " is a responsibility, my friend. It is a burden, my soul ! Franci has shed tears over it, the tears of a poet. You have read of Apollo, at least you have heard of him, the god of poetry, of music, of grace ? yes ? Behold him, Colorado ! He lives before you, in the form of Franci. Come on, that we, clean together the brasses ! "

As for the monkeys, they at once adopted John as their companion and their lawful prey. They climbed over him, they tried to get into his pockets, they nestled in his arms, they challenged him to races among the yards. The Skipper was their king, Franci was their model, the ideal toward which they vainly aspired, Rento, good, homely Rento, was the person who fed them, and with whom they could take any liberties, with no danger of a beating ; but the new-comer, the boy John, was simply another monkey like themselves. Dressed up, it was true, like men, but in no other way resembling them more than another, more than themselves. Let him come and play, then, and put on no airs. These were the sentiments of Jack and Jim, and John responded to them with hearty good-will.

The Skipper sat smoking, and watched with a quiet smile the gambols of the three young creatures, as they sped here and there about the rigging, chattering, laughing, shrieking with glee.

"Laugh, my son!" he said to himself, between the puffs of his cigar. "Laugh and play, my little son! Far too little laughter has been in thy life so far; here thou shalt be as gay as the sun is bright on the Bahamas. Of what use to be a sailor, if not to rejoice, and to see with joy the works of God and His glory? Laugh, Colorado, the sound is music in my ears!"

But by-and-by the play must cease. Orders were given, and Rento and Franci set to work in good earnest. The wind was fair, the tide was setting out. What should keep them longer here? The sails were hoisted to the tune of "Baltimore," and Rento's gruff bass and Franci's melting tenor were mingled for once in friendly harmony.

> "I wish I was in Baltimore!
> Io!
> A-skating on the sanded floor.
> A long time ago!
> Forever and forever,
> Io!
> Forever and forever, boys,
> A long time ago!"

Just as the cables were about to be cast off, a hail was heard from the wharf, and Mr. Bill Hen Pike appeared, purple and breathless.

"Schooner ahoy!" he gasped; and then fell against a post and mopped his brow.

"Señor!" responded the Skipper, coming to the stern,

and greeting his guest with a wave of the hand, "you come to bid us farewell? It is kindly done! Or you bring us, perhaps, a message from our revered uncle? Speak with haste, Señor, the tide waits not!"

"I — I brought this!" said Mr. Bill Hen, holding up a small object. "I went up into his room, to see if there was anything he might like, and there warn't nothing but just this. I thought you 'd like to have it, Johnny, to take along with you."

The good man's voice faltered; John ran to the stern, and held out his hands eagerly, tenderly, crying,—

"Oh, thank you, dear Mr. Pike! thank you so very, very much!"

For it was the china poodle that Mr. Bill Hen had brought. When the treasure was safe in the child's hands, Mr. Bill Hen breathed more freely.

"Now you 'll have something to remember us by, Johnny!" he said. "We 've lotted on ye a good deal, here to the village; more maybe than you thought on. I — I 'll miss ye consid 'able, off and on, ye see, off and on. You 'll think about us nows and thens, won't ye, Bub?"

"Oh, yes, indeed!" cried little John, eagerly. "I shall think of you a great, great deal, Mr. Bill Hen! You have always been so good and kind to me, and I shall miss you, too, and Lena, and lots of people. And — and how is Cousin Scraper, please, Mr. Bill Hen? Does he miss me, do you think?"

"He 's all right!" replied Mr. Bill Hen, gruffly.

" Doos n't seem none the worse for his tantrum. No, if you ask me, I can 't say as he seems to miss ye, not anyways to hurt him, that is. He 'll be out again to-morrow all right, doctor says ; and besides bein' rather uglier than common all day, I don't see no difference in him."

John sighed, but not very heavily.

" I suppose if I had been nicer he might have missed me," he said ; " but then, on the other hand, if he missed me, he would n't be so comfortable at my going away ; so, you see ! "

Mr. Bill Hen did not see, but he said it was of no consequence. Then, coming to the edge of the wharf, he shook hands all round, never noticing, in the pre-occupation of his mind, the knife that Franci flashed and brandished in his eyes as a parting dramatic effect. He held John's hand long, and seemed to labour for words, but found none ; and so they slipped away and left him standing alone on the wharf, a forlorn figure.

Down the river ! Sailing, sailing over the magical waters, past the fairy shores, already darkening into twilight shades of purple and gray. The white schooner glided along, passing, as she had come, like a dream. In the bow stood the Skipper, his eyes bent forward, his hand clasping fast the hand of the child.

" We go, Colorado ! " he said. " We go, my son, to new worlds, to a new life. May a blessing be upon them, as my heart feels there will be. Behold, my friend, the ways of God, very wonderful to men of the sea. I come up this river, with what thoughts in my heart? Partly of curiosity, that I see the place where my mother, long dead, was born, came to her womanhood; partly of tenderness for her memory, regard for her wish; partly, also, for anger at the villain brother, my uncle, and desire for revenge, for my rights. I come, and I find — a child! A brother for my present life, a son for my age, a friend for my heart! Living upon the sea, Colorado, a man has much time for thought; the sea speaks to him, the sky, the wind and wave. What is the word they say, each and every one, in the ear of the sailor? 'Glory to God!' That is it, my son. Let us give thanks, and begin with joy our new life together!"

Down the river! The banks fade into shadow, the breeze sinks away, but still the tide flows free, and the schooner slips along like a spirit. Now comes up the white fog, the fog out of which she came gliding that first morning; and it receives her as a bride, and folds her in its arms, and she melts into the whiteness and is gone. Was it all a dream? Or does there still come back to us, faintly borne, sweetly ringing, the song of the sailors?

For - ev - er and for - ev - er I - - o,

For - ev - er and for - ev - er boys, A long time a - go.

www.ingramcontent.com/pod-product-compliance
Lightning Source LLC
Chambersburg PA
CBHW032019010726

47493CB00007B/2483